The Trunk

C.M. CASTILLO

GLASS
SPIDER
PUBLISHING

ISBN: 978-1-957917-06-1

Library of Congress Control Number: 2022911771

Edited by L. ShoulterKarall
Cover design by Judith S. Design & Creativity
www.judithsdesign.com
Published by Glass Spider Publishing
www.glassspiderpublishing.com

Also by C.M. Castillo

The Pages of Adeena

www.cmcastillowriter.com

To my wife, Kris, whose humor and honest feedback always proves to be just what my story needs, and to my friend and editor, Laurie Shoulter Karall. Your friendship, humor, and wisdom will forever inspire me.

CONTENTS

CHAPTER 1 9

CHAPTER 2 21

CHAPTER 3 30

CHAPTER 4 39

CHAPTER 5 49

CHAPTER 6 60

CHAPTER 7 69

CHAPTER 8 78

CHAPTER 9 88

CHAPTER 10 100

CHAPTER 11 113

CHAPTER 12 129

CHAPTER 13 139

CHAPTER 14 154

CHAPTER 15 164

CHAPTER 16 175

EPILOGUE 180

ABOUT THE AUTHOR 184

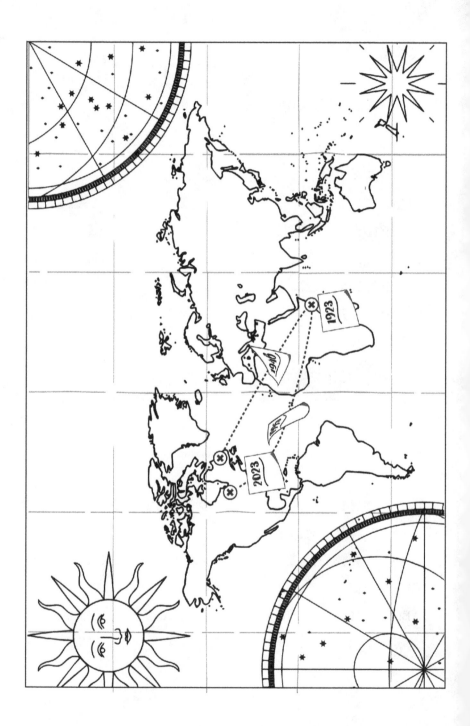

CHAPTER 1

Early Autumn, 2023

The heat, as they drove toward the consignment shop, felt unbearable to Simone. She could feel the sweat drip down her back under her sleeveless linen shirt; cringing slightly she made a mental note to never again wear linen in Florida. Only in Florida, could it be this hot and humid in September. As she reached over to turn up the car's air conditioning to its highest setting, she briefly turned toward Katherine, her future mother-in-law who sat erect and proper in her seat. Seeing pursed lips and tense brows, Simone relented, knowing that Katherine would most likely not approve. She wondered if Katherine ever perspired. At 75, Katherine maintained her striking good looks and was always impeccably dressed; her makeup was perfect, and her hair was never out of place. Next to this formidable woman, Simone, with her unruly auburn hair now up in a messy bun, lanky 5' 9" frame, and unusual golden-brown eyes, always felt awkward. No matter what she wore, or how carefully she applied her makeup or styled her hair, she still sensed that, in Katherine's view, she was merely ordinary.

Today's outing was to be a kind of reacquaintance for her and

Katherine, a new start. Michael, Katherine's only son and Simone's fiancé, had arranged the day trip after Simone had shared with him that she wasn't comfortable around his mother; she had sensed that Katherine did not approve of her. To her surprise and annoyance, Michael had simply laughed, treating her concerns as ridiculous and unfounded. To make matters even more uncomfortable, he suggested to his mother that she and Simone spend an afternoon together while they visited his family in Florida. Now, as they drove to Katherine's favorite consignment boutique for a shopping day, Simone wondered how she would ever get through this morning and the planned lunch afterward. Her stomach churned slightly from nerves and this morning's coffee. She silently thanked her good fortune that she and Michael were only in town for a few more days and would be heading back home to Chicago at the end of the week.

"Simone, would you mind turning down the air dear? I'm chilled." Snapping out of her internal diatribe, Simone quickly gave Katherine her best professional smile and obliged. "You know dear, I do appreciate you driving this morning," said Katherine, sounding slightly annoyed. "Your little economy vehicle is so much easier to maneuver through traffic than my Mercedes. Although why you and Michael chose to drive to Florida in this Lilliputian putt-putt rather than fly is beyond me." Turning to look at Katherine, Simone opened her mouth, but could not come up with a retort that sounded as smooth and effortless as Katherine's blatant dig about her compact hybrid and their decision to drive. So, instead of attempting to explain to Katherine that they drove simply for the joy of road tripping, she surrendered to the fact that Katherine, once again, had the last word.

They had been in the consignment shop for less than ten minutes when Simone concluded that The Purple Alligator was not a store she would ever wish to set foot in again. She saw it as the true definition of bourgeois Florida. Looking around at the well-displayed cocktail dresses, tennis outfits, scarves, and designer bags, Simone knew she would not be caught dead in any of these outfits. For one thing, she couldn't afford them. She simply could not believe the amount of money they were asking for consignment clothes! Glancing over the racks, she spotted Katherine in deep conversation with another woman. Realizing she must appear entirely too bored to Katherine, who periodically glanced her way, she made an effort to check out a few dresses to appear more interested. Walking over to a particularly hideous orange cocktail dress, she casually glanced at the price tag. "What the hell?!" Realizing she had spoken aloud, she quickly turned to see if Katherine had heard her shocked outburst. Luckily, her future mother-in-law was still deep in conversation. Grabbing the dress, she waved to Katherine and pointed to the dressing room. Katherine smiled, dismissed her with a flip of her manicured hand, and turned back to her conversation.

Escaping into the small dressing room, she closed the privacy curtain and sat on the stool. She hated being here with Katherine. The woman frayed her nerves. She knew the way she was feeling was partially her own insecurity around Michael's mother but dammit, she simply could not warm up to her. She was always able to read people well and she knew that Katherine only tolerated her. Reaching into her pocket, she pulled out her cell phone and punched in her best friend's number. "Answer, for fuck sakes, answer!" she whispered frantically into her cell.

"Simone? Why are you calling me? I thought you were on a shopping adventure with the Wicked Witch of South Florida?"

"Oh, real funny woman. Maggie, you are not going to believe this! Right now, I'm hiding out in the changing room of a crusty, uppity consignment shop trying to avoid Katherine's scrutiny. To make matters worse I am about to try on the most hideous cocktail dress I've ever seen, and it cost $500! It's used for Christ's sake!"

Laughing into the phone, Maggie, Simone's closest friend since the third grade, shook her head at her friend's frantic voice. When Simone finally took a breath, Maggie spoke soothingly to her friend. "Simone, hon, listen to me. Before you and Michael drove down to Florida, you promised yourself that you would do your best to get to know his mother. This week is supposed to be your bonding time with her. You know how close they are."

Exasperated and beginning to sweat in the small changing room, Simone took a deep breath. "Yes, I know...I know what the plan was Mags, but this woman's presence reduces me to a ten-year-old child. I swear I may start crying the next time she says something nasty to me." Suddenly noticing the sweat from her palms was making the dress damp, she gasped. "Oh, fuck Maggie, I'm sweating on this ugly $500 dress. I've got to go. I'll call you later." Simone clicked off her cell and did her best to smooth out the wrinkles created by her perspiring fingers. "I frigging cannot believe this! Christ!" she whispered. "Maybe if I hang it back up immediately, they won't notice." Leaving the changing room, she decided she needed to get out of The Purple Alligator as quickly as possible; she felt like a bull in a china shop. She did not want to handle another item for fear of somehow damaging it.

Seeing Katherine browsing through the racks of dresses, Simone straightened her shoulders and quietly cleared her throat. As gracefully as possible, she walked over to where Katherine stood. "Katherine, if you don't mind, I think I will wait for you outside. I noticed there are some small tables on the plaza. Please don't rush; take your time shopping. I'll just grab a coffee."

Looking up at the taller Simone as if she were a stranger asking for a hand-out, Katherine let out an exasperated sigh. "Well, yes dear," Katherine droned, "if you must." Now squinting at Simone, Katherine appeared contemplative. "I thought you'd enjoy the shop, but clearly, the prices are a bit out of your range. So, yes dear, I will meet you outside at the café once I've finished my shopping."

Cringing slightly, Simone did her best to appear unaffected by Katherine's remark. "Please take your time, Katherine, I'm not in a hurry." Giving Simone a curt nod, Katherine turned without another word to continue her browsing.

Leaving the shop, Simone felt her nerves immediately calm. She breathed in deeply, exhaled, and made her way to the plaza. "That woman makes me want to drink, but I'll settle for coffee," she said, walking the short distance to the coffee shop. After purchasing her iced latte, she spotted an empty table outside in the shade, which was protected from the sun by a colorful umbrella. "Perfect," she said. Settling in with her drink and cell phone, she dug into her bag to pull out her day planner. Smiling to herself, she knew she was considered old school by her colleagues. As a fundraiser for a non-profit healthcare organization specializing in helping low-income communities, she juggled many clients and needed the hands-on attention to detail and easy access that a day planner added. She was meticulous about every event, meeting, and call. Most of her colleagues did not use a day planner any longer; they had all their appointments and notes logged into their smartphones. Simone however, loved writing her notes longhand, noting details such as what kind of coffee clients preferred for their events, how they wanted their meetings set up, which caterers to hire, all the things that helped her clients know she was there for them 100 percent. Because of her attention to the smallest details, she was one of the top fundraisers in the business, and several new clients had asked for her by name based on the feedback from other enthusiastic philanthropists. She knew she owed her attention to detail and expertise to her brilliant mentors who had taught her that to be successful, one must care, really care, about the goals that their clients strived to achieve. She did care, and she told herself that she'd always remember that lesson. Smiling, she jotted down some notes specific to her next fundraising project, an infant vaccination awareness initiative geared to young single mothers in Chicago's low-income neighborhoods. Assuring herself that all details were in place for the next week's client meeting, she stretched out her legs and slowly drank her coffee.

Without the scrutiny of Katherine to fray her nerves, she relaxed and enjoyed the solitude, yet her mind soon moved to thoughts of the next day's dinner at Michael's parents' estate, and an introduction to his extended family. Closing her eyes, she took a deep breath and a sudden pang of sadness and melancholy enfolded her. It was a now-familiar feeling, nagging at her and becoming a constant over the past few months. Bowing her head, she allowed herself to analyze these feelings. Sitting in the heat of the Florida sun, she could not stop herself from believing that, with her engagement to Michael, she was somehow compromising the life she has always believed she was destined to live. Thinking back, she recalled that fateful day when she was twelve, looking up at the fluffy white clouds in the bluest of skies, and eating ice cream on the back stairs of her family's home. She had suddenly known that she had a special providence; she knew her destiny. In her certainty, she had looked to the sky and smiled; it was as if a kiss from the universe had touched her cheek. Her assuredness of her future had led her to her desire to help people, to a career in nonprofits, and to the belief that there was someone special with whom she would spend her life, her soul mate. What had happened to that certainty for her future?

Hearing a loud noise, Simone turned toward a sight that made her laugh in surprise. Standing in front of a small shop window, with the name Metamorphosis in bright white script elegantly displayed above the shop door, was a little man dressed as an elf. He wore a dark green jacket with silver buttons and matching hat, and even wore opaque green tights and black silver-buckled patent leather shoes. Now, struggling with a large planter, he was huffing and puffing so loudly that Simone, fearing he'd have a heart attack, felt compelled to help him. Jumping up, she threw her planner in her bag and quickly made her way over to the little man. "Excuse me, would you like a hand with that? It looks a bit heavy." Simone asked, already helping the little man by steadying the planter that appeared in danger of tipping over.

Looking up at Simone, the little man smiled broadly. "Oh! Yes, yes, please. Thank you! I must place these planters in front of the shop. Today is our grand opening, and I am already running late in preparing." Simone liked this strange little man immediately. His broad dimpled smile was genuine, and his eyes were kind and the most unnatural color green, like an ocean. With her help, they quickly moved one additional planter and placed it in front of the small shop.

Turning to the little man, she asked. "Is there anything else I can help you with?"

Looking around as if he forgot something, the little man placed his hand on his chin, appeared reflective, and then smiled. "No, no, I think that's all I need. But will you come in and see our shop? It's quite nice." Charmed by his easy manner, Simone smiled broadly and nodded as he led her inside.

Feeling a cool breeze as soon as she walked through the door, Simone smiled; it felt like a spring day inside and she breathed in the scent of fresh-cut flowers. She scanned the shop, surprised at

how spacious it appeared, and how beautifully each item was displayed. Earrings, necklaces, and bracelets made of jade, amber, silver, and other metals were positioned on a canvas to showcase
their intricate details. Delicate china vases in cobalt blues and deep
greens were bursting with colorful lilies and irises. There were por-
traits in exquisite frames and an assortment of music boxes that
played small snippets of baroque music, unbelievably, in sync with
each other. In awe of the unusual beauty of the shop, Simone wandered slowly through the seemingly endless array of objects.
Browsing the racks of clothing, she leaned over to look more
closely at a woman's bomber jacket hanging on an ornate coat rack.
It was a soft brown leather and had a winged insignia stitched on
the shoulder. Taking the jacket from the rack, she held it up, admiring its appearance. Seeing the monogram *A.M.E.* stitched on
the breast of the jacket pocket, her eyes widened in amazement.
"What in the world?" she blurted out. Hearing the little man humming, she turned to see him walking toward her. "Excuse me," she
said, a bit unbelievingly. "This couldn't possibly be Amelia Earhart's jacket, could it? Because that would be, well, remarkable."

Placing his hand on his chin as he had done earlier, he seemed
to be thinking. Finally, looking up at Simone, he smiled. "It is a
very smart jacket, is it not? Please, why don't you try it on? It seems
to be your size, and I'm sure Amelia won't mind a bit," he said with
a wink. Smiling, Simone slipped the jacket on and, as she thought
it might, it fit perfectly. Walking over to a decorative floor-length
mirror, she gasped at her reflection. Of course, it was her, however
her normally auburn shoulder-length hair seemed brighter and
fuller. Her bright golden-brown eyes sparkled, and she stood taller,
more erect, as if she were beaming with a new confidence. She
couldn't pull herself away from her reflection. "It definitely suits
you," said the little man, pulling her out of her wonderment.

"Would you like to purchase it? As today is the grand opening, everything is on sale. I can sell it to you for, let's say, $20."

Simone, returning from her complete surprise at how this jacket made her feel, turned to look at the little man in astonishment. "$20? Did you say $20? Are you serious? For this amazing jacket that couldn't possibly have belonged to Amelia Earhart, you want to sell it to me for $20?"

Helping Simone remove the jacket, the little man hummed. "Why yes, no one else could do this jacket justice but you, my dear, other than Amelia, of course," he said with a smile. "Now come and look at a few more items I think you might be interested in before we ring you up." Following the little man, Simone realized that she didn't know his name.

"Excuse me, I'm Simone. Simone Adan." She smiled. "May I ask, what is your name?"

"Oh! Forgive me, my dear. I am Henry, at your service." Bowing slightly, he reached for Simone's hand, smiled, and gently shook it. "We have quite the collection of historical items toward the front, Simone." Smiling, he waved for her to follow as he started to walk toward the front of the shop. Stopping in front of an array of colorful scarves and hats, he bowed again. "I'll leave you to browse at your leisure. Just come see me if there is anything you fancy."

Simone watched in amazement as he walked toward a tall desk and hopped up onto a swivel stool. Staring, she was enthralled by the unusual sight of the little man in the elf suit holding a quill pen and humming as he twirled in his seat and concentrated on his work. Shaking her head, she looked at her watch. She had only been in the shop for fifteen minutes. Strange, it felt as if she had been there at least an hour. Regardless of the time, she knew she needed to get back to The Purple Alligator to meet Katherine or there would be hell to pay if she kept her waiting. Deciding to purchase the jacket and quickly leave, she made her way toward what she assumed was the sales counter when she noticed a large steamer trunk in the corner near a window. It was perfect, she thought, to use for a coffee table. She had been half-heartedly looking for the right piece for her condo's living room for months, but nothing seemed right. She knew that this trunk would fit perfectly. It was in excellent condition too. Crouching down, she looked closely at the trunk, taking in its details. It was a deep dark yellow, subtle and not bright. It had worn dark brown leather straps with bright silver buckles. There were a few stickers plastered to it from Madrid, Peking, Buenos Aires, and Africa. Simone could picture it being loaded onto a large steamer ship. She wondered if the stickers were authentic. Looking closer, she noted faint stamp marks. "Holy shit," she whispered, "These *are* real!" She knew then, at that moment, that she had to have it; this trunk would be hers. Turning quickly, she searched out Henry. "Henry! Henry are you here?"

As if summoned by the queen, Henry appeared. "Yes, Simone, how may I be of assistance?"

Taken by surprise at his instantaneous appearance, Simone cleared her throat and smiled. "I think I may want to buy this trunk. However, I have a small compact car…"

"Oh! Not a problem, we ship all over the world. We can certainly ship this purchase to you."

Simone walked over to the trunk and reached out her hand to gently caress the leather straps. "I love this trunk." Attempting to lift it by its handle, Simone grunted at the unexpected weight. "Henry, can you please open it? There's something inside."

Looking questioningly at Simone, Henry sighed. "Oh, no, I cannot unlock it. You must purchase it as is; those are the rules." Looking curiously at Henry, but not questioning his remark,

Simone simply nodded. A few minutes later Simone had made arrangements with Henry to have the trunk shipped to her Chicago address. Saying goodbye to the little man, Simone stepped out of the shop. The sun shone brightly, and the heat felt unbearable on her skin. Turning, she was relieved to see that Katherine had just stepped out of The Purple Alligator. Thank goodness, it was perfect timing.

*   *   *

The trendy upscale bistro with its hip music and extravagant prices was out of Simone's comfort zone but she knew that Katherine was making a statement. A statement that said, "This is my life and it's Michael's life too. Can you handle it?" The servers knew her by name and waited on her as if she were royalty. Even the owner came by to greet her. Once lunch was served, no fewer than five people that Katherine knew had come over to the table to say hello. Simone was introduced by name, not as Michael's fiancée, a slight that Simone knew was meant to hurt her. "Tell me, dear, how is your job coming along? Michael tells me you work for a nonprofit charity. Honestly, that can't pay much. I understand you have an advanced degree. I have contacts in Chicago who can help you secure a position making more money than you could ever make at a nonprofit."

Looking up at Kathrine between bites of her shrimp scampi, Simone carefully formulated her reply. Katherine was obviously not a fan of Simone, but she was still Michael's mother and Simone knew she needed to be respectful. "Thank you, Katherine, I do appreciate the offer. However, I am quite happy with the organization I work for; they are gaining ground with their efforts to assist low-income families in the Chicago area. We have been very successful over the past twenty-four months, and our outlook for 2024 looks promising."

Putting down her fork, Katherine looked at Simone for a moment, then lifted her glass of wine to her lips and took a drink. Simone waited. "A word of advice dear," Katherine said, draining her glass and then snapping her fingers to get the attention of the server, whom she asked to bring another wine. "Michael will take over the Florida dealerships. We have groomed him from an early age. He will also be relocating from that Midwest ghetto you both currently live in, back to Florida. You'd best think about that before you get too cozy with your current career choice." Bending close to Simone, Katherine practically seethed. "I'll be damned if I'll allow my son to stay in that crime-plagued city that he currently calls home."

Stunned at Katherine's outburst, Simone was at a loss for words. Who was this woman? She was like a lioness protecting her cub but protecting him from what? Just as she was about to counter Katherine, their server arrived to check on them. Looking at him with an impossibly serene smile, Katherine asked for the bill and then promptly stood and walked off to powder her nose, leaving Simone with no choice but to pay for their meal.

CHAPTER 2

Unlocking the door to her condo, Simone stepped in, breathed out a long sigh, and stretched, feeling a satisfying pop in her lower back as the tension she had been experiencing was released. She was exhausted, physically and mentally, from both the long laborious drive back to Chicago and the events of the past week. Walking into her living room, she threw her purse on the couch and turned to make her way to her bedroom, trailing her suitcase behind her. Lifting it onto the bed, she began to unpack as her thoughts moved to the disaster the past week had been. She should still be in Florida. Instead, she and Michael weren't speaking, and she was certain that Katherine now held a much more negative opinion of her than she previously had. She looked down at the jumble of clothes. Exasperated, she decided to let it all go for now. All she wanted at that moment was to open a bottle of her favorite wine, sit back and not think.

Abandoning her unpacking, she made her way to her kitchen and reached for a Merlot. Uncorking the wine gave her a sense of calm. Being home alone was what she needed at this moment. She poured the wine and sipped it slowly. Taking in the tart fruity taste, she leaned against the kitchen island thinking about the disaster that she knew would end her engagement.

She and Michael had been in Florida for less than two days when things had begun to unravel. Katherine had been pushing her buttons since she had arrived. First there was the disastrous shopping day and lunch, and then the dinner party fiasco. Simone had known that Katherine had reservations regarding her and Michael's engagement, however, until recently, she had no clue of the depth of his mother's desire to see an end to their relationship.

To Katherine's utter disappointment, Michael had not chosen a woman of their own proud Cuban heritage. Instead, he chose a half-Mexican, half-Spanish American as his fiancée. The fact that Simone held two advanced degrees and was a top performer in her field offered no esteem in Katherine's view.

They were attending a dinner party at Michael's parents' home. Katherine had already had a few glasses of champagne before she and Michael arrived. Simone sensed an underlying burn in Katherine as she walked over to greet her. It had made her extremely uncomfortable, and she found herself on guard. As soon as Michael left her side to speak with his father, Katherine wasted no time sharing her true feelings.

"I'm sorry, Simone, didn't Michael explain that this evening's dinner party was cocktail attire?" Katherine wasn't the least bit sorry, and her bored and slightly drunken gaze oozed her disapproval of Simone's outfit, a pale-yellow cotton sleeveless dress, and flat tan sandals. Caught by surprise by Katherine's direct hit, Simone was temporarily at a loss for words. "Really, Simone, must you always be so average?" Turning, Katherine waved to a few newly arrived guests and walked off.

Simone watched her glide through the small group as if she were the fricking Queen of Sheba. Trying to wrap her brain around the reasons Katherine disliked her so much, she didn't notice when

Salvador, Michael's father, approached. Smiling, she did her best to let Katherine's insult go as she greeted him. Salvador Romero was a tall, elegant man. Simone found him kind and genuine. He always seemed sincere and Simone felt at ease in his presence. "Simone, you look lovely this evening. Would you like a glass of champagne?" he asked as he handed Simone a crystal glass of the bubbly wine. Taking the drink from his outstretched hand, Simone smiled. "Thank you and, as usual, you look dashing." Laughing heartily, Salvador bowed slightly.

"Simone," Salvador said simply, taking a sip of his whiskey he looked directly at her. "My wife is a very proud woman. She was not born into this life and has struggled a great deal, making her way by pure determination and will. She has never allowed anyone to beat her down, and that will has hardened her." Looking at him, Simone was curious as to why he felt he needed to share this information with her.

"Salvador, there's no need," Simone said, putting her hand on his arm.

Taking another sip of his whiskey, Salvador once again looked at Simone. "My words are by no means an excuse or an apology for my wife's behavior. I simply wanted to share a glimpse into the world of your future mother-in-law." Smiling at Simone, he raised his glass. "You are a lovely, intelligent young woman and I hope my son proves worthy of you. Now if you will excuse me, I see a business associate I must greet." Simone watched him walk away and felt the evening could not get any stranger.

Soon enough she realized, she could not have been more wrong. After the evening meal and light dinner talk, Simone felt more relaxed. Walking into the garden, she scanned the space looking for Michael as she was ready to leave and return to their hotel. So far, she had avoided any further confrontations with Katherine and did not want to push her luck by staying at the party any longer than was necessary. Seeing Michael in deep conversation now with his mother and several other guests, she realized that leaving early wasn't an option.

"Come and join us." Michael waved Simone over to the small group that looked to be in deep discussion. As Simone approached the group, she immediately noticed Katherine entwine her arm with Michael's and pull him closer to her, as if staking out her property.

"Simone," said Katherine. Simone inwardly cringed; Katherine looked like a cat ready to pounce. Looking at the petite woman directly, Simone felt certain Katherine was going to attempt to trip her up. "Dear, we were just discussing the deplorable situation at the border. It really is sad that all these poor Mexicans are making the choice to come to our country. They should stay where they are and work hard to make something of themselves. Instead, they are straining the resources of the United States. Seriously, ever since this president has been in office, the situation has become so much worse."

Needing a few moments to process what she had just heard from Katherine, Simone blinked a few times and cleared her throat. She knew Katherine wasn't so crass as to believe what she had just said. She knew Katherine wanted her to react to her words and cause a scene, therefore justifying her opinion of her in front of Michael. No, she reminded herself, I will not allow myself to fall into an embarrassing trap set by this woman.

Speaking in a strong steady voice with no hint of malice, Simone looked directly at her future mother-in-law. "Katherine, it is my understanding that you yourself came to the United States as a refugee. Am I correct?" Katherine's face turned dark at Simone's words, but she said nothing. Simone continued, "When it became

24

clear that Castro would implement a communist government, your family left with only the clothes on their backs and made their way to the shores of the United States." Turning now to Michael and Salvador who had joined the group, she spoke with a level of respect that she felt for the strong Cuban people who braved the journey to a world they did not know. "I believe if it were not for the assistance of the United States government, many of your country's people may not have survived, and perhaps would have even been turned back. Surely you would afford the same to the many refugees at the southern borders?"

Not waiting for a response from the group, Simone turned to Michael, who now stood staring at her. She was not surprised to see anger in his gaze, and it was anger at *her* she knew. Anger for speaking to his mother in such a way. She knew then that Michael would never have her back; his mother would always come first. "I'm tired. I'm sorry everyone, but if you'll excuse me, I think I will head back to our hotel. Michael, are you coming?"

Looking at Simone, Michael did not hesitate. "No," Michael said, in a cold voice. "I'll stay here, with my family." Pulling her to the side and out of earshot of the others, he held tightly to her arm. "How dare you speak to my mother that way? You have embarrassed me and honestly, it's best that you do leave. We will discuss your behavior later at the hotel." With that, Michael walked away and returned to his mother's side. So, there it was, she realized. Michael had chosen his mother over his fiancée. She wasn't surprised, only sad.

When Michael had returned to their suite later that evening, they had a terrible argument that ended with him leaving and returning to his parents' home. After much contemplation and a sleepless night, she had phoned Michael in the morning to let him know she would be driving back home to Chicago immediately.

Her call went directly to his voicemail. Later, he texted his reply, telling her to have a safe trip home.

Now, savoring her favorite wine back in her condo and able to process the events of the past few days, Simone felt relieved. Relieved not to be in Florida, relieved not to be under Michael's disapproving mother's microscope, and relieved that Michael had stayed behind with his family. "What am I doing?" she said. The realization that she and Michael were just not compatible and had drifted in different directions was painfully clear. So clear that, at this moment, she could not believe she had not seen it sooner. It was as if a switch flipped in her brain. The feelings she had experienced with Michael's mother, the judgment and disapproval, were the same feelings she had felt from Michael over the past few months. She rubbed her forehead and groaned loudly; it was all too much. Hearing her cell ring with Maggie's familiar tone, Simone reached for it. Biting her lip, she answered. "Maggie, hi."

"Hey, how are you? Are you home? Why did you leave Florida? You're meant to be there bonding with Michael's immensely inappropriate mother."

"Oh, Mags, don't kid. It was a disaster."

"Tell me what happened." Maggie now sounded sincere in her questioning. Simone knew if anyone would understand and not judge, it would be Maggie Clark, her bestie, sharer of secrets, and the horrible first drags of cigarettes and sips of stolen beers behind her parents' garage.

"I'm sorry I left you hanging with only a text saying that I was heading home. I needed the alone time to think. I couldn't stay, Mags." Simone said as she felt tears beginning to form. "It was clear to me that Katherine hated that I was there with Michael. I know that this was meant to be a week of bonding, but there is no bonding with that woman, and Michael did nothing to discourage her from her verbal attacks. The final straw came at Thursday's dinner party; she purposely tried to get me riled up. Oh, hell, what does it matter? Anyway, I simply couldn't stay after that and honestly, I was not too surprised when Michael decided he would."

"Wait, what are you saying, Monie? What the hell did that witch do?" Simone had to smile at her friend's use of her childhood nickname whenever she became exasperated. "Michael didn't reel his mother in? For fuck's sake! Now you are saying he didn't return with you; he's still in Florida with mommy dearest?"

Beginning to feel the pressure of the conversation, Simone's head throbbed with a dull pain. "You know how it's been with Michael and me over the past few months; we're not connected. We haven't been connected for ages. I've begged off invitations to hang out with him and his friends for dinners and parties. They just don't interest me; we have nothing in common. At first, he was upset. Now, well, it's as if he's relieved that I'm not with him, and honestly, so am I." Taking another sip of wine, she breathed out. "Mags, I can't marry Michael. I can't. I…I don't love him. I thought I did once, but now I'm certain I don't." Simone closed her eyes and tears slipped down her cheeks.

"Simone, listen. You should speak with Michael as soon as possible." Maggie's voice was calm and supportive in Simone's ear. There were no incredulous shrieks, no trying to talk her out of her decision, merely a matter-of-fact reality in her tone. "You'll need to be upfront with him, Monie. Tell him tomorrow if you can. I know discussing this serious situation on the phone is not perfect. But, if he is in Florida with his parents, you have no choice."

Simone felt grateful, grateful for her wonderful friend and her non-judgmental response. "Mags?"

"Yeah?"

"Thank you. Thank you for your unwavering support, you really are my rock."

"Simone, I have been your wingman since the third grade, and you mine. You and I have had each other's back through every conceivable fuck up since then. We have survived, and you will survive this as well. I trust you to know your own mind and heart. If you tell me you don't love Michael, well then, I believe you, and I'm here for you."

Sniffling as she took another sip of her drink, Simone sighed. She didn't say anything for a few moments. She simply wanted to be silent, secure in the cozy bosom of Maggie's loyal friendship and love.

Swallowing to clear her throat that felt raw from emotion, she suddenly thought of the only bright spot in the entire otherwise dismal trip, her discovery of the small consignment shop run by Henry. Thinking about the funny little man with the sea-green eyes made her smile, and her heart lifted just a bit. "Before we hang up, I want to tell you about this bizarre experience I had while I was in Florida. It was so unusual that I can't stop thinking about it." Sensing Maggie's interest, she continued. "I had the oddest experience while out shopping with Katherine. It was…for lack of a better description, it was as if I had stepped into another world." Thinking about what she had just said, Simone laughed lightly. But honestly, she could not describe it any other way.

"Okay. I'm listening, explain please." Simone smiled. She could hear the curiosity in Maggie's voice. She shared every detail regarding Metamorphosis and the little shopkeeper, from meeting the strange and charismatic little Henry to walking into the most charmingly fairy tale-like shop she had ever experienced. She even went into detail describing her feelings of confidence when she put on what couldn't possibly be Amelia Earhart's bomber jacket. Finally, she shared her unusual draw to the steamer trunk and her subsequent purchase of it for use as her coffee table.

Maggie chuckled at Simone's description of Henry and the small shop and couldn't stop herself from teasing her friend. "Monie, you'll never outgrow your love of fairy tales, will you?"

"Nope, most likely not," Simone said, smiling.

* * *

The dream felt like reality, as her dreams often did.

Walking on a beach, Simone could feel the soft warm sand between her toes and the stinging coolness of the waves that came up onto the shore. The sky was a blue that didn't exist, turquoise with gold and amber flecks, cloudless and bright. As she walked, she lifted her head to catch the fresh scent of the sea. Turning full circle, she put her hands to her brow to block the sun to see more clearly. She could see someone walking toward her. She felt an anticipation and an excitement she couldn't comprehend. As she continued to gaze toward her visitor, her hair became caught in the wind and obstructed her view. Pushing her hair away, she lost sight of the person. A sudden sadness overcame her at the loss. Just as she was about to turn and walk further down the beach, a soft hand gently touched her arm and she looked up into beautiful gray eyes, the color of a stormy day, and a gentle smile that she knew was meant for her alone.

CHAPTER 3

The jarring shrill ring of her cell woke her out of a deep sleep. Moaning at the intrusion, she reached for her phone on the nightstand and clicked on the call without bothering to identify the caller. Still drowsy from sleep and the memory of the intense dream, Simone mumbled a halfhearted hello.

"Simone, I'm back in Chicago; we need to talk." Michael's voice was pinched, angry and, Simone could sense, frightened. "I have several important meetings this afternoon that I cannot cancel." Sounding exasperated, he suggested they meet in the park across from his office at 10:00 a.m. Looking at her cell, she saw it was nearly 8:00 a.m.; she had a couple of hours to mentally prepare herself for what she would be sharing with him. Taking a quick shower and dressing in jogging pants and her favorite DePaul alumni t-shirt, she sat at her kitchen island and absently stirred her coffee.

What was she going to tell him? They had dated for over two years and had been engaged now for three months. What could she really say, that she didn't love him, that she probably never had? Would she tell him that over the past several months she felt herself drifting away from him? She knew he had sensed the change, the disconnect. They had begun to spend less and less time together, they were seeing their separate friends and attending different events and they rarely made love. One rare night, when their connection seemed to have come back to the days of their early love affair, they had excitedly decided to become engaged. Thinking about that night now, it was most likely a last-ditch effort by both of them to save their relationship. Putting her head in her hands, Simone knew she still cared for Michael. He was a decent guy, bright, often romantic, and successful. But it wasn't enough, she realized. Something was missing. She knew that what was missing was the all-consuming love that took hold of you and made the world a wonderful place. She wanted to be mad for someone. She wanted to wake up each morning sighing in contentment, knowing that that special person was right there lying next to her, and she wanted passion. She never felt that with Michael, and she realized she never would.

She thought about the unusual dream she had the previous night. She had never dreamt of a stranger before in such an intimate way, with such anticipation, from her sensual smile to her confident gaze and to the feel of her touch. She was aroused she realized. What the hell? Confusion creased her forehead, and, despite these unsettling feelings, she couldn't help but be curious and intrigued by the strange and unsettling dream.

Bringing herself back to Michael, she moaned in frustration "Jeez, what a mess? How could I have been so wrong?" she whispered, feeling the loss of her relationship with both a sense of relief and a sense of guilt. Checking her cell, she saw that it was time to leave; she had forty-five minutes to get to Lincoln Park and meet with Michael. She breathed a sigh of relief that he had chosen the park to talk. She did not want to do this in her condo or his office. It would have left both spaces with the stigma of a failed relationship and she didn't want that for either of them.

Cycling on the bike path that ran along Lake Shore Drive had always soothed her, though today's silver-tinged waves, bleached by the sun's rays, gave her no solace. This morning she felt only sadness. Pedaling slowly and steadily, and in no hurry to meet with Michael, Simone absently watched as joggers and cyclists made their way along Chicago's famous lakefront. Finally, crossing onto Fullerton Avenue, she peddled the short distance to Lincoln Park and her inevitable conversation with Michael.

Walking her bike up the path toward the zoo, Simone relished the soft breeze that caressed her face and the smell of freshly cut grass. It was a lovely early fall morning in Chicago. "A lovely day for ending my engagement," she whispered in a hollow tone. Up ahead she saw Michael, handsome in his skinny suit and trendy short haircut, sitting on the bench with one knee bouncing errati-cally. She smiled sadly. He was such an attractive man, but not someone she cared enough about to spend her life with. Turning, he watched her make her way toward him. He stood, straightening his jacket as if preparing for a meeting.

"Simone, hi," Michael said agitatedly, "How was the drive from Ft. Meyers?" Simone looked at him and laughed lightly, not at all amused, but saddened by how innocuous and irrelevant his ques-tion was, like something you'd say to a visiting client.

"Can we please sit?" Nodding, Michael waited for Simone to sit before joining her. Both turned at the same time toward one an-other. Michael took a deep breath and appeared to deflate. He reached for Simone's hand. She let him take it; his hand was warm and strong, and she couldn't help but feel sadness for the loss of what they once shared. "Michael," she said, "I...I am so very sorry our trip to Florida turned out as it did. I had hoped that your mother and I could connect. I really wanted that and I hope that you know that is the truth." Looking closely at Michael, his face was a stoic mask of neutrality. Only his eyes gave him away; a mix of anger and sadness welled up in his dark brown gaze. He *knew*, she realized with surprise. He knew that she was going to end their relationship. Clearing her throat, she paused momentarily to collect herself. She and Michael's two-year relationship had taught her that Michael's expressions were telling and, right now, he was telling her without words that he knew their relationship was over.

Suddenly pulling his hands away from Simone's, Michael spoke. "Simone, don't." Shifting his weight, he moved closer to her. "I…look, I know what you are about to say. I am not as dense as you think," he said half smiling. Clearing his throat, he looked at Simone with affection. "I know that we have been drifting away from each other for months now. I watched it happen and I didn't try and stop it. I didn't try because, well…I questioned if we really loved each other." Simone could see that he was trying to maintain his composure. "I think we both realize that we don't," he said finally. Dropping his head to his chest, Michael was silent.

So, there it was. Simone looked at Michael's lowered head. Who was this man, one minute pompous and selfish, and the next sparing me by speaking the words that I find so difficult to say? She had come to break it off with him, and he knew it. So, instead of her saying the words that would hurt them both, he voiced them. Looking down at her hands, she moved to gently remove her engagement ring. Holding it in two fingers for a moment, she looked at it and then placed it in Michael's palm. "I wish that we could have…well, that we could have been the one for each other," she whispered. Reaching over, she put her arms around him, holding him tightly. Wiping the tears from her cheeks, he kissed her gently, stood up, and walked away.

The Trunk

* * *

"So, when is this amazing trunk going to be delivered?" Maggie asked as she rifled through Simone's refrigerator for a bottle of water. It had been two weeks since Simone and Michael had ended their relationship. To Simone's relief, Maggie had looked at her sad face and decided that they needed a regular jogging regimen to get them in better shape. Simone was grateful for her friend. Now, their early morning bi-weekly exercise helped clear her head, and Maggie's company was always a blessing. Back after the morning's jog along the lakefront, Simone busied herself making coffee and putting out a breakfast of scones and fruit. The day was chilly and a bit overcast, but their run had been good and they were both pleasantly exhilarated from their pace.

Taking a large gulp of water, Maggie smacked her lips. Looking at her, Simone snorted at the goofy look on her friend's face. With her short, naturally blond hair, now dyed sky blue and sticking up in all directions from the exertion of their run, no makeup, and a too big cut-off running shirt, Maggie looked like an adorable pre-teen. As she handed her a cup of black coffee, Simone chuckled and ruffled her hair. "You look like a twelve-year-old Smurf wearing Papa Smurf's t-shirt."

"Hey, you! Leave my hair alone." Maggie laughed, playfully pushing Simone's hand away. "My kids love it. They think their teacher is the coolest in the school. Yum, I love your coffee," Maggie said as she drank and reached for a scone that Simone had put out on the kitchen island.

"Maggie they're six years old," laughed Simone. Shaking her head, she had to admit that Maggie did look very trendy and cool most days, though right at this moment she looked like a kid. "Okay, okay, your students are very hip for six-year-olds. Of course, they're correct. You are the coolest teacher in the school."

Smiling, Maggie bit into her scone. "So," Maggie said, as she wiped crumbs from her hands and lifted her fingers to mimic air quotes, "the magical trunk, when do you expect it to be delivered?"

"It's not magical. It's simply a very cool piece of history," Simone said, sipping her coffee. Looking toward the bare spot in front of her couch, she smiled. "It'll be perfect as my new coffee table. It's funny though, when I first spotted it, I just knew I had to have it. It was such an intense feeling. Isn't that strange?" Simone said thoughtfully. "Anyway, it should be delivered this Friday. It took a few extra days, something to do with the weight being more than the delivery company anticipated."

Thinking suddenly back to the day, nearly three weeks prior, when she had purchased it, she recalled that when she had attempted to lift it by its leather strap, its weightiness surprised her. Henry had said that they were not allowed to unlock it to see what was inside, that she must purchase it as is, that those were the rules. "Huh," she whispered softly, grabbing Maggie's attention. Lifting her brows and gesturing for Simone to explain, Maggie finished her scone.

"Well, as I said, the trunk caught my eye. It was such an interesting piece. I could picture it making its way through faraway places, being carried by broad-shouldered men as they made their way through jungle paths. Intrigued, I reached over and attempted to turn it around so I could inspect the back and the sides. That was when I felt how heavy it was. I literally could not move it." Maggie, now at full attention, waited for her to continue.

"Yep," Simone said absently, "It was very heavy, as if it were completely filled." Simone was just about to tell her what Henry had said about not being allowed to open the trunk when Maggie excitedly jumped off her kitchen stool.

"Simone! You could be rich! It could be full of money! Think of it. Maybe it's loot from a bank robbery from the Roaring Twenties. Oh, no, wait—it could be bootleg money from prohibition!"

Nearly spitting out her coffee, Simone burst out laughing. "Maggie! You goofball! There is definitely something wrong with you. I'm pretty sure that there is no secret stash of cash in that trunk. Please stop." Looking at Maggie and shaking her head, she continued to laugh. "And you have the nerve to say I believe in fairy tales!" Laughing herself, Maggie plopped back down on her stool and sighed loudly.

Simone leaned against the counter and thought about the weight of the trunk. "It is strange, but I don't have a clue of what could be inside. When I bought it, Henry said that I couldn't open the trunk until I purchased it, that that was the rule."

"The rule? What does that even mean?"

"Honestly, I have no idea."

"Okay, this is crazy and weird, and honestly, super exciting! You said the trunk will be delivered Friday? Well, I'm coming by, so don't make any plans," Maggie said enthusiastically. Simone raised her eyebrows and nodded, thinking of Henry's cryptic message.

* * *

Simone sat out on her balcony looking over the city she loved. Living on the twelfth floor allowed her a good view of downtown Chicago and the lakefront. She had lived in Chicago all her life and never got tired of the beautiful city by the lake. Like any large urban area, it had its share of problems. It took a lot of cooperation amongst its citizens and strong city management to recover from the pandemic that had started in 2020. However, they were making strides each day, and she had faith that they would flourish as the

City of Big Shoulders once again. Very little noise from the streets below filtered up, so she felt comfortably peaceful. Her balcony was small but not confining. She had decorated it with a cozy love seat, side table, and several potted plants to help give it a feeling of tranquility, as well as to obstruct the view of her neighbors' balconies. She had also strung soft white lights across the top. It was her little bit of heaven. Sitting now on her loveseat with a glass of wine, she breathed in deeply and let her breath out slowly. She thought of Michael. They had talked only once since their breakup, and it was simply to sort out belongings and return keys. It was such a mundane ending to a relationship she initially believed would be perfect. She thought of their first meeting, a blind date, set up by a mutual friend.

Simone had not had high expectations. When she and Michael first met, she hadn't dated men for a few years. Actually, other than a few casual dates with women, she hadn't really dated much at all. She had been so focused on her career that she hadn't allowed herself time to think about much else. Meeting Michael and connecting with him was a surprise. They had clicked, or so she had thought. As they moved through their courtship, they had fallen into a routine. A comfortable routine that she now knew she had mistaken for love. Looking out toward the lake, Simone took a sip of wine and wondered what had happened to her. A light melancholy moved through her now at the realization that somewhere along the way, she had settled. She told herself now that she would never allow routine to dictate her life again.

It was humbling that, once she had let her family and friends know that the engagement was off, no one appeared to be surprised. Had she and Michael been the only ones who were clueless? Sipping her wine, she looked at the night sky; the quarter moon was bright and reflected on the water as the gentle movement of the waves helped ease her sober mood. She was content to be here in her own space, knowing that she had finally made the right decision, even if it had taken a trip to Florida to visit Katherine for her to realize it.

As a yawn escaped her, she stretched and decided to call it a night. Making her way into her living room she reached for the lamp to switch off the light and briefly eyed the empty space in front of her couch. She thought of the trunk she purchased, visualizing it in her living space. It was such an interesting piece, beautiful in its detail and in such amazing condition for something she assumed was over one hundred years old. She found herself excited about it; she knew it would suit the space well. Switching off the other lights, she made her way to bed.

CHAPTER 4

"**S**imone, you up? Simone!?"

"Maggie, jeez, what time is it? We're not running today. Why are you calling so early?" Simone yawned and looked at the clock; it was 7:00 a.m.

"Because it's Friday. That's why I'm calling. So, what time do you expect the trunk to be delivered?" Simone sat up in bed and yawned again as she moved her cell to her other ear, laughing lightly into the phone. "Seriously, how can you still be asleep? Will the delivery service contact you once they deliver it?" Simone laughed again at Maggie's exuberance. Attempting to pull her brain out of its still sleep-affected stupor, Simone briefly wondered why people always seemed to call at the crack of dawn.

"Maggie, really? You're calling me at 7:00 a.m. to ask about the trunk? Could this not have waited until, oh, I don't know, noon?" Hearing Maggie laugh, she chuckled herself. "Okay, if you must know, I think the delivery service is dropping it off at 4:00 p.m. this afternoon. Eddie, the condo maintenance man, said he will bring it up to my door so no worries about trying to move it ourselves."

"Okay, that's great, I'll be by after school. I have parent-teacher conferences tonight until 6:00 p.m. Jeez, I hate these things. So many parents believe their kids are perfectly behaved little Einsteins, but there I'll be, ready to burst their bubble." she said with a laugh. Simone smiled. She knew Maggie was an excellent teacher and was only joking. Her students meant the world to her, and she worked with each one to ensure that they received the attention and support necessary to be successful. Simone was in awe of her dedication and admired her friend's commitment to what she knew was an important step in the development of these young minds.

After they said their goodbyes, Simone got out of bed. Her first meeting wasn't until late morning, so she had plenty of time for coffee and a long shower. Tuning in her favorite morning radio station, she started the coffee. Just as she was about to jump in the shower, her cell rang again. This time it was her sister, Annie.

"Simone, it's me. I've had another dream and you know how prophetic they can be."

Simone sighed. Ever since her younger sister Annie had been hit on the head by a falling pot of petunias at the age of ten, she'd insisted that she had psychic abilities, although, to date, nothing she predicted, as far as Simone knew, had ever come to fruition. Now, ironically, as a successful floral designer with her own shop, Simone often wondered if it was the falling petunias that had given Annie her green thumb.

"Annie, why are you up so early? Don't you usually sleep until noon?"

"Oh, har-har, smarty pantalones. No, I do not. I'm on my way into the shop. I have three early morning clients, two weddings, and a funeral." Annie laughed at her own small joke. "Actually, sis, I called to check on how you're feeling after the debacle with Michael, and to tell you about the dream I had."

Sighing into the phone, Simone paused; she did not want to

discuss her feelings again about her broken engagement, especially on the phone with her very chatty baby sister. She knew Annie was concerned but she had already explained that she was fine. Actually, she was good. She had no regrets about ending her relationship with Michael.

"Annie, hon. I'm fine, honestly. Both Michael and I are good with our decision. Truly, you know I'd share with you if I weren't." Simone meant it too. She was very close to Annie; they often spoke and confided in each other.

Sensing that Simone was sincere and that her sister did not want to discuss her break-up any further, Annie changed the subject. "Okay, you know I'm here if you ever need me. So, sis, there's another reason I called. As I mentioned, I had a dream, and this dream, well it was all about you." Annie heard Simone's soft groan of exasperation. "Simone, please listen. I had the dream a while ago but wanted to wait to tell you about it until, well, a little time passed, and things weren't so raw. It was so detailed; I feel it's important that I share it with you. Why don't you come by the shop tomorrow? I'll order lunch and tell you everything."

Taking a moment, Simone was about to decline but then conceded. Lunch with Annie would be nice as she hadn't seen her sister since her return from Florida.

*   *   *

After a long hot shower and two cups of coffee, Simone headed to the office. Her mind wandered to Henry and the cryptic message he had shared with her the day she purchased the trunk. Henry had said that she would need to purchase the trunk as is, that those are the rules. "Those are the rules," she said to herself, "What does that even mean?" Now, to add to the strangeness of the past several weeks, there was the bizarre discussion she had with Annie earlier. Annie, who believed everything that happened was predestined, had dreamt of her and the dream had apparently affected her enough that she felt she needed to share the details with Simone in person. Maneuvering her way through traffic, she told herself to get a grip; she was starting to get carried away like Maggie, who dreamed of stolen loot and prohibition-era mysteries. Switching on her Bluetooth, she allowed the sounds of Billie Holiday to help calm her racing thoughts.

As luck would have it, her day was frantic with many unexpected problems. Client meetings were canceled or rescheduled, a vendor who was typically reliable was late due to their own staffing issues, and Simone's assistant called in sick with the flu. By 4:00 p.m., she was nowhere near done for the day. She had to reschedule several meetings and she needed to contact several vendors regarding orders. Looking at her cell, she decided a quick call to Maggie was warranted. She didn't want to get frantic calls from her while she was trying to speak with clients. After leaving her a voice mail letting her know she wouldn't be home any earlier than 7:00 p.m., she got back to work.

*   *   *

Driving home with Chinese carryout from Chang's and a bottle of chardonnay, Simone switched on her car's playlist. Ella Fitzgerald's smooth voice filled her ears as she neared home. Ella always calmed her, and she knew that, after today's frantic pace, she needed to relax. Realizing that Maggie would be waiting for her when she entered her condo's lobby, she groaned. She was tired and didn't want to deal with Maggie's excitement regarding the trunk right now. The trunk could wait, she thought. She was hungry and a chilled glass of chardonnay sounded heavenly.

"Simone! There you are." Maggie jumped up from where she sat in the lobby to help Simone with her packages. "I went up to your floor to see if the trunk arrived. It's in front of your door in a huge crate. Eddie said that once you got home, let him know, and he'll grab the dolly and move it into your condo."

Handing the wine and one of several bags to Maggie, Simone greeted her with a peck on the cheek and said hello to the doorman who smiled from the front desk. "Honestly Maggie, I'm beat. Let me settle in and then I'll call Eddie." Exiting the elevator on her floor, Simone gasped. Sitting in front of her door was a huge wooden crate with her name and address stenciled across the entire front. "Oh, wow, that's humongous. I don't remember it being this enormous. Do you think it will fit through the door?" Both women stared at the massive wooden box for several seconds.

"Yes, yeah, I think so, once it's out of the crate. Let's call Eddie now."

Simone nodded, pulled out her cell, and punched in Eddie's number. After an impressive production of crowbar, dolly, and a lot of grunting, Eddie was finally able to uncrate and move Simone's trunk into her condo. "Miss Adan, that's one heavy trunk, but it sure is a nice looking one," Eddie said as he wiped sweat from his brow.

Simone looked at Eddie and felt bad that he had such a hard time uncrating and moving the massive trunk. "Eddie, wait, before you leave let me give you a tip." Simone reached for her purse and pulled out a twenty.

"Thanks, Miss Adan, appreciate it. Let me know if you need anything else," he said as he walked out the door of her condo, still mopping sweat off his brow.

Simone locked the door after Eddie left and turned to Maggie.

"Behold, my new old coffee table trunk. Isn't it amazing?"

Walking toward the trunk, Maggie slowly leaned down to look closely at the worn, faded stickers. Reaching out, she caressed the silver strap buckles as she continued to gaze intently at the over-sized trunk. She eyed the metal lock that kept the trunk secure. Grabbing it, she pulled a few times. It wouldn't open so she looked up at Simone.

"Did Henry send a key?"

"I don't know," Simone said, holding the manila envelope that had been taped to the top of the trunk. She tore it open. There was no key. The only thing in the envelope was a handwritten note in beautiful script on crisp parchment paper. It simply read,

Enjoy the journey. A leap of faith can lead to amazing things.

"Simone? What does it say?" Simone looked at the note again and then handed it to Maggie. Reading the note, she looked back to Simone. "Okay, I think I need a drink. Do you want to crack open that wine?"

Simone, still a bit stunned, nodded and moved to her kitchen to grab the wine opener. She stood there thinking. The note had said, "Enjoy the journey." What journey? Grabbing two glasses, she walked back to the living room. As Maggie continued her inspection of the trunk, Simone picked up the note again; she stared at it for a moment before she laid it down and poured a glass of wine for herself and Maggie. "We need to open this lock," she said suddenly. Bending down to inspect it, Simone announced, "This cannot be that difficult to open." Both women eyed the lock closely. "A locksmith, you think?" said Simone.

After several rings, a message played, and Simone clicked off her cell. Turning to Maggie, she said, "They're closed. I'll call again tomorrow."

"Can't you leave a message saying it's an emergency?" Maggie asked as she took a healthy drink of her chardonnay.

Looking incredulously at her friend, Simone shook her head. "They did have an emergency number but opening a trunk is not an emergency. Can you imagine me interrupting these people with that message at this hour? It's not going to happen. We can wait." Looking at Simone, Maggie smirked an embarrassed grin, making them both break out in low laughter.

*   *   *

That evening, Simone lay awake in bed contemplating Henry's mysterious note. She knew he had written it; it seemed like something he would do. The entire experience of Henry and the shop was so bizarre; it was like a Grimm's fairy tale. She smiled thinking that Annie would have a field day with this mystery. Sitting up suddenly, she switched on her bedside lamp. "The bomber jacket!" she said. "I completely forgot about the bomber jacket." With everything that had been going on, she hadn't thought of it since she hung it up in the closet when she returned from Florida. Getting out of bed, she walked to the closet and flipped on the light. Looking at the jacket, hanging in the garment bag Henry had placed it in, she could not believe that she had forgotten how different she felt when she had first tried it on. The jacket's effect on her had baffled her the first time she wore it but now she realized that its strangeness was simply part of her experiences since she had stepped foot into Henry's shop.

Gingerly removing it from the garment bag, she caressed the soft dark brown leather of the jacket. It was supple, as if it were well-worn and broken in, yet it looked to be in pristine condition. Carefully removing it from its hanger, she held it up. It had a faint smell of jasmine that she had not initially noticed. It was a smart-looking jacket. She could still not believe Henry had only asked $20 for it. Holding it to her chest in front of her full-length mirror, she slowly stretched out her arms and slipped it on, pulling up the collar. Feeling a sudden rush of chilled air, the tingling built and vibrated through her limbs. She sighed contentedly. After a moment, she peeked at her reflection. Taken aback, her brows rose with amazement and curiosity. It was her, of course, wearing the jacket over her oversized t-shirt in her bare feet. But the amber flecks in her eyes were bright and full of humor. Her hair was a deep chestnut brown, shiny and rich. Her cheeks looked healthy, and her lips were a soft pink and full. She looked confident and, if she cared to admit it, she looked intriguing and…the only word that came to mind seemed ridiculous; she looked sassy.

She laughed aloud at that thought and her voice sounded different somehow. It was hers, but richer and deeper. Standing there, she almost convinced herself that she was dreaming but she knew that she wasn't. Quite unexpectedly, she realized that she was seeing herself as the person she knew she was, the Simone Adan she felt she was in her heart. She stood for several more minutes contemplating how this strange garment made her feel. Running her hands slowly over the jacket to smooth out the seams, she suddenly felt something she hadn't noticed before. It was small and situated near the upper left shoulder. She quickly removed the jacket and felt carefully along the inner seam. There! A small hidden pocket, secured with fine thread. Carefully removing the thread, she reached in and removed a small metal key. She stood for several moments simply holding the key and looking at it. The key, she concluded, must be the key to the trunk. It had to be; it couldn't be anything else. She brought it over to the light of her table lamp. It looked ordinary enough, shiny, new, a key to a lock. Turning it over in her palm, she breathed deeply. Her first thought was to run to the trunk and open it, but she felt apprehensive. What if it were simply filled with old books, nothing that would help her understand what was happening? Her disappointment would be immense. No, I need a bit of time to absorb the situation. Tomorrow...I will try the key tomorrow.

She laid the key on her nightstand. Picking the jacket up from the chair where she left it, she walked to her hall closet and hung it amongst the jackets and coats she regularly wore. "There," she said. "Now I won't forget about you; you'll be right here where I can find you." Walking back to her bedroom, she once again looked at herself in the mirror. She noted that remnants of the confident woman she had seen when she put on the jacket remained. Smiling, she lay down on the bed and closed her eyes, dreaming once again of the beautiful stranger.

She was sitting at a small table at a café somewhere, but it definitely wasn't Chicago. Her hair whipped in the strong breeze and the air smelled like fresh-baked bread. Smiling at the fragrance, she took a deep pull of air and savored the aroma. She was waiting for someone she realized; she could feel the excitement, the anticipation of her presence. I haven't seen you for so very long. Will you really be here in a few moments? Will I really see your beautiful face and deep gray eyes smiling at me? She took a drink of her espresso; it was hot and strong, and it jolted her. A child floated by in a blue dress, smiling and waving. She waved back. Across from where she sat, a river flowed. Its strong yet gentle current carried ducks and geese and a beautiful turquoise blue and yellow bird that surely could not exist. As she marveled at the unusual creature, she felt a presence approaching, an exciting, beautiful, magnificent presence. Her heart raced and she was filled with such a sense of anticipation; it nearly took her breath away. It was her. She knew it had to be, finally. "I've waited so long...but who are you? Who are you?" she said.

Waking with a start, Simone looked around to ground herself. The morning sun was streaming through her bedroom window.

Breathing hard, she ran her fingers through her hair. It had been another dream. "Who are you?" she whispered. Closing her eyes, she visualized the stranger and tried to recapture the dream in detail. The familiar feeling of the excitement and anticipation of seeing the woman returned. She caught her breath and the need to be with her coursed through her every cell. She groaned. "I really need to get out of this bed."

Turning toward her nightstand, she looked for a long moment at the key that lay exactly where she had left it last night. Biting her lip, she wondered why she felt so apprehensive. She should be running over to the trunk now and unlocking it to see what was inside. After all, it belonged to her; she had purchased it. "No, I need time to digest everything that is happening. I need time to decide on my next steps," she said emphatically.

Getting out of bed, she moved toward her bathroom to take a quick shower, but not before she picked up the key and carefully placed it in a small silver box on her dressing table.

CHAPTER 5

Annoyed for not better managing her time, Simone found herself running late for her lunch date with Annie. She hated being late, being prompt was a big deal for her. Although, she had to admit, recently she'd been late more often than on time. Her focus had been off ever since she stepped into Metamorphosis. She was very aware of this fact. It was all just so strange.

Driving south toward Annie's floral shop in the Pilsen neighborhood, her thoughts lingered on last night's dream and finding the key in what couldn't possibly be Amelia Earhart's jacket. It had thrown her for a loop. She couldn't stop thinking about it. The dream had frightened her, the poignancy of its energy, the disappointment she had felt upon waking, and the realization that her rendezvous with this mysterious stranger was simply a dream. And, what of the key? Finding it in a jacket she had purchased at the same shop where she'd bought the trunk was simply not a coincidence. Taking a long breath, she attempted to clear her mind. She checked her dashboard clock and shook her head. She would just need to accept that she'd be late and do her best to relax. Despite her hurried start to the day, her morning client meeting went well, but it had run slightly over due to her client's excited comments and their need for more details. Luckily, her sister was easy-going. She knew she would not be perturbed by Simone's tardiness. As close as she and Annie were, she had decided to hold off on sharing the details of Henry's shop and her purchase of the trunk, at least until she could grasp the strangeness of it all herself. She could imagine Annie's excitement overwhelming her. She visualized Annie holding a séance to resurrect the long-gone original owner of the trunk. "Oh, good lord," she said. Shaking her head and smiling, she maneuvered her way into the parking lot of the shop.

The Violet Bloom always put a smile on Simone's face whenever she entered. She took a deep breath; it smelled heavenly. The scents of lilies, mixed with roses and hydrangeas, filled the lovely bright airy floral shop. Seeing her sister with a customer, Simone waved hello and busied herself with browsing; she wanted to take some fresh flowers home to place on her new coffee table.

"Do you see something you like?" Simone turned and smiled when she saw Annie walking toward her. Annie was slightly shorter than Simone's 5'9". Although they shared the same coloring, Annie had two big dimples on her cheeks that made her look exactly like a younger version of their mother. "Hey sissy, how are you?" Annie said, giving her a big hug, which Simone happily returned.

"I'm good, and how are you, little sis?" Simone said, picking up a vase of colorful daisies. "I think I like these best, they're so festive." Calling over her employee, Anita, Annie asked her to wrap up the bright bouquet for Simone to take with her when she left.

"I'm awesome, business is fab. Come on, let's go to my office and have lunch, I'm starved." Annie led the way, chatting happily. "Honestly Simone, large orders are coming in just about every day. Business has been amazing!" she said as she opened the door to her office and reached for a brown paper sack on her desk.

Opening the bag, she pulled out two wax-paper-wrapped sandwiches. "Caprese for you and roast beef for me," she said as she handed Simone her lunch. "Sit," she said, gesturing to a cozy leather chair next to the window. Walking a few steps to a small fridge by the door, she pulled out two bottles of water and handed one to Simone as she plopped down in her office chair.

"I'm so glad you're here," Annie said as she unwrapped her sandwich. Looking at Simone, she said kindly, "You've been a bit elusive lately. Honestly sissy, should I be concerned?" Annie watched Simone as she busied herself with her own lunch and waited. Simone said nothing.

Sighing, Annie continued, "Okay, I won't pry, but I would at least like you to know I am here for you. You are my big sis, and I love you." Simone looked lovingly at her sister, smiled, and grabbed her hand, squeezing it affectionately.

"So, will you allow me to share my dream with you? I think it's important." Simone looked at her sister and shook her head no as she uncapped her water. Looking exasperated, Annie asked, "But why not? Don't you want to know what might be in your future? Simone, I am offering you something that is unprecedented." Looking closely now at Annie, Simone could see that she was frustrated.

"Annie, hon," Simone said, putting down her bottle and looking directly at her sister. "Thank you, I really mean that from my heart, but honey, your dreams…well they haven't actually been helpful to me over the years."

Watching Simone for several minutes, Annie looked at her sheepishly and then sat back in her chair and laughed. "Well, yes, I suppose they haven't been for you, have they?" Biting her lip, Annie said, "I've always been sorry about that. Hah! Do you remember when we were in high school, and I told you I had that dream that Jason Rivera was going to ask you to Junior prom? You begged Mom to buy you that dress for the dance and you even bought fake eyelashes, and then Jason never asked you. He asked that new transfer girl. Jeez! You were so pissed at me," Annie said with a giggle she could hardly control. Simone laughed too, nearly spitting out her lunch.

"Shit, Annie, that was so awful. I don't think I spoke to you for a week after that," said Simone, laughing about it now all these years later.

"Okay, okay, I get why you don't want to hear it, but, over the years, I have honed my skills. I don't often have dreams that I feel have significance but honestly, more times than not, the small things I feel or dream come to fruition in some way or form." Leaning toward her sister, Annie looked sincere. "I swear I wouldn't be sharing this with you if I didn't have such a strong feeling about this, please believe me."

Seeing her sister's sincerity, Simone sighed and relented. "Okay, I suppose it can't hurt to listen to what you have to share. After all, our prom days are long behind us," she said, laughing. Smiling, Annie took another bite of her sandwich and nodded. "But let's eat our lunch first, I don't want to lose my appetite," Simone teased.

After they had finished their lunch and caught up on the family, Annie decided to close the shop early. Giving Anita the rest of the day off, she locked the door and poured them each a small snifter of aged brandy before stepping over to her Bluetooth and switching on Andrés Segovia, soft and low. Watching Annie closely, Simone couldn't help but think that her sister was setting the stage. "What's going on? I feel as if you are going to whip out your crystal ball at any moment." Laughing, Annie threw her head back in an exaggerated movement and cackled like a witch. The sound startled

Simone enough that she nearly dropped her glass. "Okay, Annie, now you're scaring me."

Looking at Simone, Annie giggled, "I'm sorry, that was just me being silly. Stop looking so serious. Relax, you don't have any more meetings today, do you? I thought we could just hang. I want to hear how you're doing, you know, feeling, after the breakup with Michael, and then I will tell you about the dream I had."

Sitting back comfortably, Simone took a sip of brandy. She felt the sweet heat of the liquor slide down her throat, its taste pleasant and fragrant. Looking at Annie, she smiled. "I'm fine hon, I'm doing surprisingly well. It's funny, I initially thought it would take months for me to come to terms with ending our engagement, but it hasn't. It's been less than a month, yet I feel no real sense of loss. I think we both knew we were about to make a huge mistake. I'm just glad that we ended it before we went through with a marriage that was never meant to be."

Simone hadn't realized she had closed her eyes. In her mind, she recalled she and Michael sitting on the bench in Lincoln Park, both ending something that never should have been set in motion. Opening her eyes now, she watched her sister who had leaned back in her chair with a quiet, thoughtful expression.

Taking a small sip of her own drink, Annie spoke. "I saw you, Simone. I saw you and Michael in a dream. You were both on a park bench and he was holding your hand. I saw you take off your ring and place it in his open palm."

Simone looked closely at her sister. There was no hint of pretense in her voice. The look on her face showed no smirk or sign that she was joking. There was nothing at all that told Simone that Annie wasn't being anything but truthful. "When did you have this dream?" Simone asked quietly.

Still displaying her thoughtful look, Annie responded. "I believe it was the night you and Michael left for Ft. Meyers. In my dream, you were wearing your DePaul alumni shirt and jogging pants." Huffing out a short laugh, Annie looked at Simone. "I thought it would be just like my big sis to wear her most comfortable clothes when breaking off her engagement. I'm sorry, I wanted to call you immediately and tell you but realized it wasn't a good time. It was only when you told us, the family, that you and Michael ended your engagement that I decided I needed to tell you."

Simone said nothing for a moment. Taking another sip of her brandy, she looked at her sister. Simone believed her; she had known what Simone had worn. This would be impossible if she had not seen her in her dream; no one but Michael had seen her that day. After leaving him at the park, she had gone home, changed her clothes, and lay in bed the entire day.

Simone's brain tried to process this new development, that her sister, who she had teased relentlessly over the years about her so-called psychic abilities, might actually possess them.

"Simone?" Turning now and attempting to focus on the present, Simone looked at Annie. "There's more."

*   *   *

That evening, in sweats and a t-shirt, Simone sat on her balcony wrapped snugly in a warm throw. She stared out over the city as she absently rubbed the small shiny key with the fingers of her right hand. The sky was clear, and the moon looked nearly full, bright with the telltale outlines of the surface faintly visible. The air felt cool and dry. Early fall in Chicago has been wonderful this year. The city tended to be extreme, with winters devastatingly cold and summers excruciating hot, but Chicagoans usually always got a reprieve from the extremes during spring and fall. Breathing in the cool night air, she thought once more of Annie's revelation. Her sister's dream had been eerily accurate, including the details of her and Michael's discussion. Then, even more unnerving, Annie had spoken of the woman, the woman that Simone had dreamed of several times over the past few weeks. A woman who didn't exist in Simone's reality, but who only appeared while she slept. She had admitted to herself that she was more than a little intrigued by this dream woman. Simone thought of her now, elegant and lovely, strong and confident. She made such an impact on Simone that, when she did appear in her dreams, she consumed her thoughts for the entire day.

Exhaling deeply, she thought of Annie's words. "Simone, I saw you; I mean, after you and Michael parted. I saw you again and you were with a woman. She was striking Simone, like a person from another time, a countess, or a movie star from the past. She had silver blond hair, shoulder-length, and wavy, amazing gray eyes, and she was tall and glamorous. The way she looked at you, watched you, it was as though no one else existed for her but you. I think my heart nearly exploded from the poignancy of it. In my dream, you and she were at a dance or a ball, I think. There was an orchestra playing and she reached out to you, and you smiled and took her hand." Clearing her throat, Annie looked at Simone, who appeared stunned. "Simone, you were so happy, a happiness I have never seen in you before."

A siren on the street below, loud and piercing, pulled her from her thoughts. "What is happening?" she whispered to herself. Deciding to try and get some sleep she stood and made her way to her living room. Locking her balcony door, she saw the reflection of the trunk in the dim light of the room. Turning, she walked toward it. It was lovely, its shiny silver buckles enhanced the soft leather of the straps. She had placed the vase of daisies on top of it, and a colorful batik adorned one side, hanging just so that any-one could mistake it for a beautiful art piece. Holding the small key in her palm, she closed her fist and held it tightly. "Not yet," she said, "not yet." Before making her way to her bedroom she gently laid the key on the trunk, next to the flowers. "Soon," she whis-pered, and then walked the short distance to her room and readied herself for sleep.

Still contemplative, and with only the sound of her own breath-ing disturbing the quiet of her room, her thoughts once again re-turned to the afternoon's discussion with Annie. How could her sister's dreams be so similar to her own? Annie's description of the beautiful blond mirrored her own memory of the woman whom she'd dreamed of over the past few weeks. Finding no explanation that satisfied her, she became restless. Deciding sleep wasn't going to come anytime soon, she got out of bed and walked to her kitchen to make herself a hot cocoa. Hearing the telltale sound of Maggie's ring on her cell, Simone reached for her phone.

"Yo, Monie, whatcha up to?" Simone could tell that Maggie had her on her car's Bluetooth and that she was driving way too fast.

"Slow down, Mags." Laughing loudly, Maggie didn't say any-thing, though Simone could tell from the sound that she had revved down her engine. Maggie loved to drive fast and she never drove anything but a manual transmission. She loved the control of shifting gears.

"So, my friend, why are you calling me at 11:00 p.m. on a Friday night? Didn't you have a hot date this evening?" Simone said, as she mixed the cocoa with milk and stirred it slowly on the stove.

Hearing a sardonic moan, Simone's eyebrows rose as she waited to listen to what Maggie was about to share. "It was hardly a hot date. As a matter of fact, there definitely won't be another with David." There was a slight pause in Maggie's voice as she shifted gears. "You know, Monie, I don't get it. Why can't a man simply be himself instead of trying that macho bullshit act? The first date David and I went on had potential. He was funny, sweet, and shy. I thought, okay, this guy is nice. Yeah, I could get to like him. So yes, I agreed to a second date. Tonight, well, let's just say that tonight was not what I had hoped it'd be." Sighing deeply and letting out a cynical laugh, Maggie shifted gears again. "So, what are you up to? Can I come by and cry on your shoulder?"

Grinning, Simone shook her head. "Of course, you can come by. I warn you, though, I am only serving hot cocoa tonight." Responding with a laugh, Maggie said she'd be there in ten.

"Ummm…like your coffee, this hot cocoa rocks," Maggie murmured as she kicked off her shoes and placed her legs under her on the couch. Looking at Simone in her oversized Chicago Cubs t-shirt and wool socks, she raised her eyebrows. "So, it seems you and I are just two single ladies alone on a weekend evening drinking hot cocoa." Simone laughed aloud, and Maggie soon followed. "You wouldn't happen to have any Kahlua to add to this concoction, would you?"

Smiling, Simone shook her head, "No, I do not. So, tell me, what the hell happened? Seriously, I thought you liked this guy."

"He was a terrible disappointment after only ten minutes. We hadn't even ordered dinner, and I knew there would not be a third date. The man I had dinner with this evening was not the same guy I had dinner with two weeks ago. This one was boorish and pompous. I was confused at first, so I asked him a few questions about our last date, you know, to sort of gauge his feeling about our first dinner. Get this, he said that he always tries the shy-guy act on first dates just so he can determine whether a second date is likely." Simone drew her eyebrows together, unbelieving. "I know, right? Get this, he said that he is much more worldly than that, and, if I let him, he could teach me a few things." Simone laughed out loud nearly spilling her cocoa. "Right?! Jeez, really, was this guy kidding? I couldn't wait to end that dinner. We were supposed to go to Buddy Guy's after, but I threw fifty bucks on the table and took off pronto. I didn't even say goodbye."

"Oh, Mags, I'm sorry. That sounds awful, and I am sorry I don't have any Kahlua, but you certainly deserve more whipped cream."

"Now, you're talking," Maggie laughed, "Oh, hell, Simone, it's okay. I dodged a bullet. It's not like I was invested in him." Looking at Simone now, Maggie asked, "So, speaking of relationships…"

Sitting up abruptly, Simone looked at Maggie unbelievably. "Oh, no you don't, missy! Do not go there." Simone laughed. "It is way too soon for me to even think of dating. Maggie, I know you, you have a look in your eye, stop."

Maggie giggled and waved her hand. "I'm just saying."

"So, what are you just saying? Tell me," Simone said, not really wanting to hear what Maggie had to say about her love life or lack of one.

Sitting back on the couch sighing, Maggie smiled. "Well, Simone, there were those girls in high school, and a few lovely ladies you dated in college, and of course Beth…Maybe you should try batting for the other team again."

Looking closely at Maggie now, Simone burst out laughing. "Oh, for fucks sake, I am not ready to date anyone. Be serious. Michael and I just ended our engagement and you're suggesting I go out and find a woman? Don't you think I should wait at least a month before I go out scouting babes?" Maggie chuckled and clinked mugs with Simone.

"Simone," she said suddenly. "Is that what I think it is?" Reaching over, Maggie gingerly picked up the key that Simone had placed on the top of the trunk. Holding it up, she waited for her to respond.

Looking at Maggie, Simone let out a deep breath, came around to the couch where Maggie sat, and plopped down next to her. Taking the small key from Maggie's hand, she held it between her thumb and forefinger. "I found this in what couldn't possibly be Amelia Earhart's jacket. There was a small hidden pocket and when I opened it…well, this was in it. I haven't tried it, but I have no doubt this key will fit that lock."

Both women stared for a few moments at the key in Simone's hand, then, as if in sync, each turned their gaze to the lock on the trunk. Simone then turned to Maggie, whose eyes were as wide as saucers, and nodded slowly. Moving off the couch, Simone knelt and placed the key in the lock.

CHAPTER 6

Early Autumn, 1923

Vivian Oliver lifted her beautiful face and laughed delightedly. Her silvery blond locks cascaded across her cheek as her steely gray eyes smiled and teased. Champagne in hand, she toasted her friend, "Bravo, Rafael, you sing beautifully. You could surely have given Caruso a run for his money darling, bravo!" The room erupted in laughter and applause. Being a dear friend of Vivian's, Rafael knew her well enough to know she was completely sincere. He knew she loved his voice and that was all that mattered to him. He beamed with gratitude and affection.

"Darling Viv, thank you for that sweet, yet well-deserved, compliment." His handsome face lit up with hearty laughter.

Caught up in Rafael's revelry Vivian jested, "Dear Rafael, humble as ever." After the applause quieted down and the guests moved about and mingled with one another, he came to stand by Vivian and her most recent companion.

"Ladies, lovely to have you join us this evening," Rafael said as he bowed slightly and reached for their hands to kiss each in turn. Vivian's companion for the evening, a sultry flapper with blood-red lipstick and striking hazel eyes, giggled and blushed. "Vivian darling, who is this lovely creature here at your side?"

Vivian, already regretting that the pretty young flapper was there as her date, smiled and introduced her to Rafael who definitely had an eye for beautiful women. "Rafael, why don't you ask Saundra to dance? I'm sure she'd be delighted, wouldn't you, dear?" Vivian said as she looked at Saundra's eager face. Nodding excitedly, Saundra allowed Rafael to gently take her arm and lead her to the dance floor.

"You know, darling, Rafael will sweep her off her young feet and you'll never see her again." Vivian turned to see her dear friend, the elegant Countess Alexandra of Luxemburg, one of the elite European aristocrats who had wisely relocated to the States to avoid the unrest brewing in Europe. Vivian smiled at Alexandra and clinked glasses with her.

"That's what I am hoping, dear Alex," quipped Vivian. Alex laughed gleefully at her friend, her soft brown eyes smiling at Vivian's words.

After kissing Vivian on the cheek, Alex looked closely at her. "Darling, why are you here? It's not that I'm not happy to see you but, when last we corresponded, you were in the Congo or some such remote place, completing your research. Yet, here you are, back home in New York with this lovely little creature who you obviously, as you Americans say, do not give a hoot or holler for. Do explain, please."

Shaking her head, Vivian pursed her lips. "My sweet dear Alex, always straight to the point."

"But of course, darling! Why beat around the bush? So, tell me, what is going on? You do realize that I can always tell when you are restless. I also know that the little bit of fluff that was hanging on your arm is not someone who will intellectually challenge you."

Laughing, Vivian sipped her champagne and then sat the glass on the tray of a passing server. "Come, Alex, let's walk out into the garden. There is a cool breeze." Vivian slipped her arm through her friend's as they walked down the path on Rafael's impressive estate. They walked for several minutes, neither woman speaking.

"I've decided to leave for an extended time," Vivian said quietly. "I've taken a commission with The American Museum of Natural History here in New York. They've read my work on Southern Kenya's ancient indigenous population and have offered me an opportunity to do more research for their ancient cultural artifact department." Still quietly strolling arm in arm, Vivian turned to Alex and smiled. "They're picking up the cost of the trip. This is quite the opportunity." Alex said nothing for a moment but turned to look at her friend skeptically. "Oh, Alex, please don't look at me that way, darling. I'm quite excited to be taking this trip. Excluding the time for the voyage, the expedition will be approximately eight weeks, and I will be working with world-renowned anthropologists and archeologists. It's what I've dreamed of, and I feel incredibly fortunate to be included."

Alex, who so far hadn't uttered a word, looked up toward the sky and sighed. "Vivian, darling, I adore you, but I need to ask, why are you running away again?"

Looking dumbfounded but resigned to answering her friend, Vivian halted as she turned to her. "I am not running away. I simply have an opportunity that I cannot pass up. This research is key to my next published work. You are well aware that my goal is to obtain a tenured professorship at the University of Chicago. Once my research is complete, I can finally publish. That will be my foot in the door at U of C."

"So, this decision to travel halfway around the world has nothing whatsoever to do with one Constantina Fararra?"

Sighing disgruntledly, Vivian looked at her friend. "No, absolutely none!" Vivian said. "Oh, Alex, why must you be so suspicious. I'm leaving because I have been given a fabulous opportunity that I simply can't pass up."

"Well, if you say so," said Alex skeptically.

*   *   *

After assuring Saundra that it was fine with her that she stayed at the party and, after obtaining a promise from Rafael that he would ensure that Saundra made it home safely, Vivian said her goodbyes to Alex and a few other friends. She ordered a cab from Rafael's upper Westside home and made a graceful, yet undetected, exit. It was not her normal modus operandi, however, she felt leaving this way was best under the circumstances. After her conversation with Alex, she felt drained. No matter how much she loved her friend, she simply did not feel prepared to share with her all her reasons for wanting to leave the country. Sitting in the taxi, she put her head back and rubbed her temples. She could feel a headache forming; all she wanted to do was get home, take off her heels, and relax. Once the taxi dropped her off, she made her way up to her apartment, breathed a sigh of relief, kicked off her heels, and sat back on her lounge. She would have liked to have a Scotch but felt that she had quite enough to drink tonight. Thinking now how this evening's soiree at Rafael's had been flowing with champagne, she smiled; whoever had thought prohibition would stop the consumption of alcohol has yet to see the New York party scene. She decided to have a cup of tea; tomorrow would be a busy day.

*   *   *

Hearing loud ringing, Vivian nearly fell out of bed. The sound was so unusual that it took several moments to comprehend that it was her newly installed telephone. Reaching for the receiver, she offered a quiet hello.

"Miss Oliver, this is the operator. Will you accept a call from a Mr. Allen with Johnson's Movers?" Responding yes, she learned that the movers would be at her apartment at 10:00 a.m. the next morning to pick up her trunk for delivery to the Port of New York for the following day's voyage.

Hanging up the receiver, Vivian leaned back. She hadn't slept well and now felt the remnants of her restless night. Willing herself to get out of bed, she threw off the blankets, stood, and reached for her dressing gown. She had a full day ahead of her. She needed to pack for her voyage as the movers would be arriving first thing in the morning. Reluctantly, she left her bedroom and made her way to the kitchen. She needed coffee in the worst way. It was a bright sunny morning and, despite her lack of sleep, she was excited about her upcoming trip.

While preparing her morning coffee, she thought of the previous day's conversation with Alex. Alex had wrongfully assumed that she was upset about her breakup with Constantina. That reasoning could not have been further from the truth. She cared about Connie, yet not enough to think beyond their few titillating months together. In the end, the lovely Spaniard was just as sure that their relationship would be short-lived, and they had parted friends. Smiling, she thought about the exquisite Connie and how they had said their goodbyes. Savoring the memory of their last lovemaking, she silently wished her well. She wondered why she hadn't shared the details of that parting with Alex; they shared many personal stories. It was, after all, an amicable ending. Thinking more about it, she knew why she hadn't. Alex would have seen through her and queried her about her restlessness and inability to connect with women on a deeper level. She had no answer to give. She wanted more. She was deeply disappointed to realize that Connie wasn't the one. She wondered if she would ever know real love. Staring out the window, she slowly sipped her coffee and recalled last night's vivid dream. She had dreamt of the stunning woman with the beautiful smile again. This had made several nights over the past month. Shaking her head, she wondered for the hundredth time if she could possibly be real.

She had been walking somewhere near a river in a charming city, one she was not familiar with. The breeze was soft, and the air had the familiar scent of recent rain. She walked with excitement and an anticipation that brought a soft smile to her lips. It was a beautiful day, and she lifted her head to scan the bluest of skies. She was meeting someone. As she approached a small café, partially hidden by large oaks and a lovely garden blooming with color, she saw her. She knew instinctually that it was she who she was there to meet. The realization took her breath away.

As she slowly walked toward her, she could see that she was lovely. Poised and sleek as she sat with a steaming espresso. Her smile was clever, and Vivian could tell that she was waiting for someone simply by the way she held herself. Suddenly, a soft breeze whipped the woman's hair around, and, with an elegant hand, she pulled the long waves into a knot atop her head. Vivian caught her breath at the beauty of her long neck, mocha-colored and inviting. She appeared so unusual to Vivian, as if she had come from a different time and place. As dreams often do, the vision had ended too soon.

She woke up before they could meet. Despite the abrupt ending to her dream, Vivian had shuddered with strong, intense feelings, and a fierce passion. Now, as she watched the day unfolding from her window, she wondered who she was, this woman who would appear to her as she slept. When she first dreamt of her, she was certain they must have met at some point. She began to seek her out at gatherings, events, and at the university where she taught, but nothing came of her searches. She started to wonder if she even existed. "Who are you?" she whispered. "Why do you come to me? Are you real?" Exasperated, not understanding what these dreams meant, she placed her empty cup in the sink. "Okay," she said, "enough! You have a lot of packing to do."

* * *

Her huge steamer trunk sat empty except for the photographs she had carefully secured to the inside of the trunk's lid. Looking at them always gave her a sense of joy and brought back beautiful memories. The photos represented many of her travels, the beautiful sky of the Savanna, the friendship she shared with her aged neighbor Madeline in Paris, the lovely evening at the Met with Rafael and Alex. One of her very favorites was of her trip to the Orient where she stood in front of the Great Wall with her guide and friend, Bohai. Gently touching her photos, she smiled. "I will add more from Southern Kenya."

Pulling open a desk drawer, she reached for paper and fountain pen to jot down a list of all she would need in preparation for the journey. Much had been completed weeks ago, such as updating her friends and family on where they could reach her and formally requesting a leave from her current university position. Now, all that was left to do was pack. Items such as her camera, passport, and new journal would all go in her shoulder bag as she wanted these items close at hand. Her clothes for the journey, including personal items, terrain boots, research journals, and other gear, could all be stored in her trunk.

By late afternoon she had finished her packing. As in the past, and as many times as she lugged the massive trunk from port to port, she was still amazed at how much it could hold. She was grateful that she had decided to purchase it back in '17; it had served her well. Reaching for the unique lock she had designed to secure the trunk through its many voyages, she carefully slipped it through the metal clasps and clicked it firmly shut. Now, all that needed to be done was for it to be loaded onto the ship.

*   *   *

"Good lord!" she sighed. Turning onto her stomach for the second time that night, she felt frustrated. Why couldn't she sleep? It was late and she was exhausted from her full day of preparing for the long voyage. As her lids fluttered shut, she again thought of the beautiful woman who had visited her dreams. She wanted to know her; she believed that she was meant to know her. "So many questions," she whispered as she finally settled into an exhausted sleep.

She was walking. Her bare feet caressed the dew of the grass, and she smelled the scent of the wild lilacs that grew in the open fields. It was a bright evening; the light from the moon reflected off the trunks of the Poplar trees and allowed her to see clearly. She walked slowly, enjoying the solitude, the smell of the earth and the beauty of the evening. As she made her way past a cluster of trees that cleared to an open field, she could hear the sound of laughter and music. Walking toward what appeared to be a group of partygoers enjoying the evening, she saw her, the woman who had dominated her dreams over the past several weeks. Her presence filled Vivian with sudden joy. She smiled as she watched her. She thought her glorious. Her full auburn hair sparkled in the moonlight, and her smile was warm and kind. Vivian watched her as she spoke to others gathered around; her voice was beautiful and musical, profound and joyous. Heat resonated throughout Vivian's entire body at the sound of it.

As Vivian slowly and methodically made her way toward her, she noted that the woman was speaking now as if holding court; all eyes were upon her in rapt interest. She smiled at how the woman held the attention of those around her; everyone present seemed to be focused on her. Vivian observed her closely. She was so different from her own fairness. She was dark, with beautiful olive skin, lustrous dark hair, and striking golden-brown eyes that shined joyously as she laughed. Turning, she said something to a man in what sounded like Spanish, and everyone laughed at his surprise and utter appreciation of her words. As Vivian walked slowly toward the group, the woman glanced toward her momentarily, then raised her eyebrows slightly and smiled. Her demeanor was welcoming as she watched Vivian's approach, and Vivian suddenly felt an overwhelming passion that she could not explain.

Sitting up quickly, with her chest heaving and her hand on her heart, Vivian strained to see the clock on her dressing table. It was nearly 3:00 a.m. Running her hands through her hair, she tried to clear her mind. "A dream, another dream," she said, as she pulled back the covers and got out of bed to get a glass of water. Now, standing at her bathroom sink, she stared at herself in the mirror. She looked pale, and a bit spooked. "Who are you?" she said loudly. Standing tall, she breathed in, and then let out a deep breath as if clearing her head and confirming a decision. "I'm going to meet you. Somehow, I will, I simply know it; you couldn't possibly live only in my dreams."

CHAPTER 7

She was bone-tired. It had been a harrowing four-week voyage from the Port of New York to Southern Kenya. The ship had weathered everything from blinding heat to monstrous waves in treacherous storms. Adding to the strenuous voyage, Vivian's trunk had never arrived on the ship. She had been forced to wear clothes loaned to her by a few generous passengers and crew. She felt fortunate enough to secure an extra duffle with a brush for her teeth and other toiletries from the ship's supply cabin. As frustrated as she was about her trunk, she had to admit that wearing trousers and baggy men's shirts during the voyage was infinitely more comfortable than the few dresses she borrowed from the generous ladies on the ship. In any case, the captain was extremely apologetic and assured her that they would do everything necessary to deliver her trunk once she arrived at her destination.

Now, exhausted, and hungry, bouncing through Kenya's rough terrain at dusk in the back of a transport vehicle, she hoped against hope that her trunk had been located and would be waiting for her once she arrived at the campsite. The camp, she learned, was located on the coast of Southern Kenya, in an area known as Unguja. Making their way slowly through the thick untamed foliage, Vivian believed she could hear every sound imaginable, from howling animals to the crack and pop of tree branches under their vehicle. As they reached the outskirts of camp, Vivian watched in wonder and awe as tall natives in colorful red garb walked and pulled carts filled with baskets of vegetables, bamboo, and spices. This was her first experience with the legendary Maasai people. She was humbled by their elegance and beauty. Once their transport truck began to slow, several young men came running up to assist with hauling equipment and gear bags; a young boy helped Vivian jump down from the back of the truck. Along with her traveling companion, Dr. David Handler, the expedition's archaeologist, they grabbed their gear and started to make their way toward camp. As they approached the peripheries of what was clearly the excavation area, a tall man with a prominent hooked nose, tiny dark eyes, dressed in a khaki shirt and shorts, approached, and extended his hand in greeting.

"Hello, hello, welcome. We expected you earlier, no matter," he said with a snort and a wave of his hand. "I'm Dr. Samuel Escabar; please call me Doctor or Sir," he bellowed with a chuckle and another snort. Vivian wasn't quite sure that he was joking. "Welcome to your new home for the next two months, Professor, Doctor. How was your journey?" Not waiting for a response, he gestured them both toward camp. "Dr. Handler, this will be your tent. I'm afraid you'll need to partner up with one of our research students, but he assures me that he doesn't snore," he snorted.

Looking tired, and unconcerned about his accommodations, David Handler, a stocky man with large protruding ears and a genuine smile, saluted both Vivian and Dr. Escabar and then made his way into his new home. "Now, Professor Oliver," Escabar said as he placed an unwelcomed hand on the small of her back, "all the girls get their own private tents, but you will share a latrine."

"Not a problem," Vivian stated, cringing, and sidestepping his touch. She had been on various digs, and from the look of camp and the sleeping tents, this site appeared better than most. However, she wasn't sure yet what to make of Dr. Escabar. Not pleased that he was being somewhat condescending and inappropriate, she considered mentioning this to him, but ultimately decided not to; why start off on the wrong foot? Besides, she was simply too tired to deal with it at this moment.

"Professor Oliver, we have employed a few local natives to help with meal prep, washing, etcetera," he said as he walked her toward her accommodations. "We want our team working, not doing laundry. So, if you need anything, Amidah will be assisting you. You will meet her in the morning." Vivian nodded in agreement. "Oh, by the way," Dr. Escabar said conspiratorially, "Amidah is a bit of a celebrity here. She is highly regarded in her community as a sort of seer or witch doctor or some such nonsense." He laughed contemptuously. "So please, simply humor her. We don't want to upset the locals. You know how these people can be. We do, after all, need them to work for us and, as ridiculous as their primitive customs may be, we must keep them happy." His smug condescension incensed her. She knew now that Dr. Escabar was not a man she could respect. "Anyway, Professor Oliver, I'll leave you to get some rest. Until tomorrow then."

Relieved to be away from Escabar, she opened the canvas tent flap and was pleased to see a cot with clean linens and blankets, a small desk with a typewriter and paper, a camp stove, several tin plates and utensils, a bucket for water, and a kerosene lamp with a box of matches. However, what she did not see was her trunk. Dropping her gear bag next to the cot, she laid down and closed her eyes. She did not want to sleep. She needed to get cleaned up and find some food, but she simply couldn't keep herself from falling into a deep slumber.

"Professor? Professor Oliver?" Gradually emerging from a deep sleep, Vivian slowly opened her eyes. Someone had lit her lamp as there was a soft glow in her tent and the wonderful smell of cooked food. Rubbing the sleep from her eyes, she sat up. An exceedingly tall and aged native woman, in a long, brightly colored garment and headdress, stood in front of her with her hands folded as if in prayer. Her skin was weathered and leathery, but her eyes were bright and clear. When she saw that Vivian was awake, she smiled gently. "Professor, I am Amidah. I am pleased to be at your service." Vivian smiled; she couldn't help herself. She was mesmerized by the woman's stature, kind eyes, and soft voice. Her accent was lovely, deep, and smooth with a quiet cadence.

"Please, call me Vivian. I am pleased to meet you." Vivian had not been in the presence of the Maasai before and marveled at her formidable height. Swinging her legs off the cot, she stretched and yawned. "Oh, my, I'm sorry. I'm still so sleepy. I must have passed out as soon as my head hit the pillow." Vivian gestured to a camping chair, looking at the old woman, "Please, won't you sit down?" Nodding, Amidah ambled over and sat down with what appeared to be great relief. Looking concerned, Vivian moved closer to Amidah. "Are you alright? Can I get you anything?"

Looking amused, Amidah laughed low, "Thank you, Vivian. I am well. It has been a long day, and I am an old woman. Therefore, sitting now is a pleasure." Looking at Vivian's worried face, she waved her hand as if to dismiss any concern. "You must be famished child. Please, I have brought stew and bread. You must eat. You can sleep again once you have filled your stomach." Vivian's appetite kicked into gear, and she reached for the bowl that Amidah had brought. Once she had eaten her fill, she put down the bowl and spoon and looked to Amidah again.

"That was wonderful, thank you." Looking at her watch, she was surprised to see that it was close to midnight. She had slept for several hours. "Oh, it's so late, should you not be home at this hour? I hope you did not stay late to bring me food."

Laughing lightly, Amidah shook her head, "No, these are my usual hours. I will be leaving for my village shortly. It is not so far, less than a kilometer. The walk is good for me." Standing now, she pointed to a small pile of towels, soap, and clothes. "I took the liberty of bringing you a change of clothes, a pair of boots, and soap for your bath. There are two other females in camp in addition to yourself, though, at this late hour, you will find privacy. You will find the bathing tent down the short road behind your tent. Sleep well, sunrise comes early in Kenya."

Looking at the kind woman, Vivian had a lot of questions she wanted to ask, but she saw that Amidah was tired and she did not want to keep her there any longer than necessary. There would be time tomorrow. Besides, Vivian knew she desperately needed a bath and could hardly wait to rid herself of the smelly sweat-soaked clothes she had been wearing for days.

"Thank you for your kindness," Vivian said with sincerity. "Uh, Amidah, one question if I may. Would you happen to know if a trunk was delivered for me? It never made it on the ship and it contains my clothes, supplies, basically everything I brought with me for this stay."

Turning to leave, Amidah stopped and smiled once again at Vivian. "Ahhhh, yes, your trunk. I understand that it is very important to you." Looking at Vivian, she said nothing more but simply smiled, bowed slightly, and slowly left the tent.

*   *   *

The next morning, Vivian woke to a loud commotion. There were raised voices and she was certain she heard a woman crying. Quickly dressing, she made her way to where a small crowd had gathered. Moving her way through the group, what she saw frightened and angered her; a young native woman was kneeling on the ground, cowering and crying as her hands covered her face. Dr. Escabar stood over her, ready to strike with what appeared to be a riding crop. "No!" screamed Vivian. "Stop!" Running toward Dr. Escabar, she stopped in her tracks. Dr. Handler had come from the small crowd and quickly snatched the crop from Escabar's hand.

"What the hell do you think you are doing?" yelled Dr. Handler. "You were about to strike her!"

Looking incensed and shocked, Dr. Escabar glared at the intrusion. "What do you think you're doing, Dr. Handler?! How dare you attempt to undermine my authority! You know nothing of these people! I have years of experience dealing with these heathens!" Escabar spat as he looked around at the group that had formed. "I grew up in this world! I learned from my father that this is the only way you will ever be respected! These natives must learn obedience, and this is the only way they will understand," Escabar said, seething with rage. "She stole from the food tent! This will not be tolerated!"

Vivian looked at Escabar's enraged, sweat-drenched face and knew that there was more to his outrage than could be explained here at that moment. Sensing a more intense confrontation brewing between David and Escabar, she quickly reached for David's arm to defuse the situation.

"David, please come help me," she said as she led him away from Escabar. Turning to Simone, David reluctantly nodded. They quickly made their way over to the frightened young woman who was hysterical with fear.

Though she could not understand her language, Vivian knelt beside her and did her best to let her know she wouldn't be punished. "It's alright, we won't hurt you," Vivian soothed, not truly knowing if the young woman understood her. Looking up, Vivian saw Amidah slowly walking toward them through the gathered crowd. Releasing the young woman, she watched as Amidah slowly bent and gently laid her hand on the young woman's forehead; she immediately calmed. Murmuring words Vivian could not hear, Amidah soothed the frightened young woman enough so that she was able to stand up and be gently escorted back to her village. Watching the exchange with curiosity, Vivian lifted her eyes to Amidah, who only nodded.

As the crowd dispersed, Vivian stood back quietly, arms crossed, trying to comprehend what had just taken place. The young woman had been hysterical, yet one soft touch from Amidah calmed her immediately. Feeling that the situation had been defused, she decided to walk back to her tent to prepare for her morning's work when she spotted two familiar faces from the previous day's camp tour speaking with David Handler. Making her way over to the small group, they each quickly introduced themselves. Vivian learned the other two women in the camp were Susan Dickson, a student researcher, and Mary Elizabeth Smith, a professor of archaeology from Oxford University.

Hearing Dr. Escabar's angry voice once again, the group quickly turned toward where he now stood. "Dr. Handler, Professor Oliver, there is much to be done today. I suggest we get to it!" Vivian's brows creased as she watched him continue to bark orders. The anger in his voice could barely be contained, his face was a deep red, and looked to be on the verge of exploding; spittle spewed from his fleshly lips. "Dr. Handler, Professor Oliver, please meet me at the dig site in twenty minutes. I will update you on our progress." With that, he turned and walked briskly away.

"Good lord! What in the world?" Vivian said as she turned back to look at her colleagues.

Mary Elizabeth looked toward the meal tent that Escabar had just entered and said, "Unfortunately, Professor, that is Escabar's modus operandi. He treats the locals deplorably, with absolutely no respect, and he is atrocious with women, especially those who have the gall to believe they are anywhere near as accomplished as he sees himself." Looking directly at both Susan and Vivian, Mary Elizabeth warned both. "Be on your toes ladies; I truly believe if it were up to Escabar, we three," she said, pointing to herself, Vivian, and Susan, "would be on the next ship home."

After that morning's incident, Vivian spent the next ten hours at the dig site photographing and deciphering the team's findings. There was much to do with the hundreds of small fragments that required expert identification. She had no doubt that, in the coming weeks, her days would be full. Hopefully, her busy days would mean she would see less of Escabar.

At sunset, she and the other team members ended their workday. Walking toward camp with Mary Elizabeth and Susan, she learned that Dr. Escabar was not pleased that she had been hired to be part of the excavation team; this did not surprise her in the least. Once again, Mary Elizabeth suggested that she watch her back. "Honestly Vivian, Escabar is known to be rigid and misogynistic, often not acknowledging the contributions of female team members, and on occasion making inappropriate advances."

After a dinner of roast meat and yams, she made her way back to her tent to prepare for sleep. Opening her tent flap, she saw Amidah turning down her blankets and straightening up her work area. "Amidah, no need to do that. I'm fine. Thank you, however, for your kindness," Vivian said as she plopped herself into her camp chair. "Good lord, it's hot," she said, fanning herself with her hat. "It makes the day so much more exhausting, doesn't it?" Hearing Amidah's low chuckle, she acknowledged her with a grin. "Yes, I must seem a silly American to you. You have endured this heat your entire life. But please know that I am prepared to get used to it and conquer it."

Turning, Amidah chuckled again. "Child, I do not begrudge your acknowledgment of the heat. Even for us, who have lived here all our lives, it can be daunting."

Vivian was curious. "Amidah, how were you able to calm that young woman down so quickly? She appeared inconsolable."

Amidah appeared pensive. "A gentle hand can convey strength, strength within one's self. The young woman is strong; she simply needed a gentle reminder. She will be good. She will not fear Dr. Escabar any longer. He is a small man with much anger. He will not approach her again."

"But, how do you know this? He seems dangerous. What is to stop him from attempting to hurt someone else? We should report him; his behavior is criminal!" Vivian was standing now, angry for the young woman and determined to make certain that this type of incident would never happen again.

Reaching out, Amidah gently touched her shoulder and Vivian felt a warmth enter her entire body. Amidah's touch was soft, yet strong. It resonated through her like a lightning bolt, fast, powerful, and fierce. She suddenly had no anger, no fear, only calm strength, and the knowledge that justice would be served. "Sleep, Vivian. It's late, and you are very tired."

Hearing Amidah's words brought a deep, comfortable tiredness to Vivian, and she yawned. "Yes…I *am* tired. Thank you, Amidah. Until tomorrow, then, good night."

CHAPTER 8

Autumn, 2023

S imone opened her eyes and stretched. Her legs became tangled in the afghan that she used to keep warm, and she nearly fell off her couch. Untangling herself, she quickly sat up and looked around the room. She realized she must have fallen asleep as soon as Maggie had left, as the remnants of their hot cocoa sat on her kitchen island and one counter light remained on. Shaking her head to clear the cobwebs, she looked at her cell. It was nearly 8:00 a.m. The sun was streaming brilliantly through the glass balcony doors. Pulling her legs up onto the couch, she stared for a long moment at her steamer trunk. It was closed now, with the straps resecured and the lock dangling open.

It had been Maggie's presence that had finally prompted her to try the key. Having her best friend at her side had given her the push she needed to take that step. They had both stared at the trunk for an extraordinary amount of time before she had slipped the key into the lock. She had to admit that they had both been just a little bit spooked by the sight of the unlocked trunk. Recalling the strangeness of it all, she moved to the kitchen to make a pot of coffee, eyeing the trunk as she walked past it.

Cup in hand, she sat at the kitchen counter and sipped her coffee slowly to allow the caffeine to hit her brain. She simply could not understand anything that was happening to her. The trunk, Henry, the dreams, what could it all mean? As a rational woman, she knew there had to be a logical explanation. She had found a key in a jacket that could not have possibly been owned by Amelia Earhart, and said key had opened a trunk that had, since she purchased it, spurred dreams of a mysterious and beautiful woman. She wanted this entire experience to be logical, though it was anything but. Slowly walking from the kitchen to the living room, she plopped down on her couch and rehashed last night's events.

Staring at the trunk, she and Maggie had both sat on the edge of the couch while Simone slowly undid the leather straps. As she lifted the trunk's lid, the scent of patchouli, rich and fragrant, had filled the air. Turning to each other, eyebrows raised and questioning, Simone whispered, "Maggie, the trunk should smell stale and musty, yet it smells like…autumn." Nodding slowly, Maggie had agreed. With a deep sigh, Simone now thought of how extraordinary it had all been.

She recalled how they had both taken in a breath, shocked when they saw that the inside lid of the trunk was lined with smooth, taut cream-colored linen. The fabric did not appear to have a bit of wear or age; it was crisp and fresh. Pinned to the inside lid were several photographs, arranged with care. It was as if the person who placed the photos there had done so with great joy and reverence. Simone had reached out her hand and carefully touched the small black-and-white photos, admiring them. They appeared old yet were in pristine condition. However, what had truly made Simone nearly faint with disbelief was the woman in the photos. *It was her*, the woman from her dreams.

There was no mistaking her; she recognized her face immediately. It was her mystery woman. She had the same silvery blond hair and striking features. She was tall, confident, beautiful, and elegant. In one photo, she stood in front of what had to be the Great Wall of China. Another was taken in New York in front of Carnegie Hall, still another in front of a small cottage somewhere in the country, and another on the ocean. In each photo, the woman smiled. Her joie de vivre was obvious. Anyone viewing these photos could see great admiration, even love, as she held the hand of an old woman in one photo and smiled joyfully with her arm wound around the shoulder of a smiling man in another. There were no dates visible to identify the years, but Simone knew that the photos must have been taken nearly a hundred years ago by the clothes that the people were wearing.

She had attempted to hide her stunned shock by making an abrupt excuse to Maggie to end the evening. She had told Maggie she was tired and wanted to wait until the next day to look through the trunk's contents. Maggie had looked at her as if she had lost her mind. Clearly, Maggie didn't buy it and had gently taken her hand and moved closer to her on the couch.

"What's this about, Simone? You look as white as a ghost." Maggie's look of concern convinced Simone that she had to tell her what was happening. She explained that, since returning from Florida, she had been having dreams, dreams of a beautiful woman with wavy blond hair and remarkable eyes. She explained that her presence in her dreams felt real, much more than simply a fantasy. Then she had pointed to one of the photographs on the inside lid of the trunk and gently touched it. "This is her," she whispered incredulously. "This is the woman in my dreams."

*   *   *

Startled out of her thoughts by Maggie's telltale ring, Simone reached for her cell. "Maggie, have you had coffee yet? I want to get out of this condo and get some fresh air."

"No, I haven't, and I am in desperate need of a double latte. Care to meet me up at Java Jive? We can grab a to-go and walk." Readily agreeing, Simone quickly dressed and, with a hasty glance at her trunk, turned and left her condo.

Now, sitting, head down with her espresso and blueberry scone, Simone felt Maggie staring at her. They had taken a small table in the park. As it was not yet 9:00 a.m., the area was nearly deserted except for a few joggers. "Stop staring at me. You're freaking me out," Simone said, rubbing her forehead.

Maggie huffed out a sigh. "Well, shit, how can I not stare at you? You're in love with a dream woman. Did I mention she is a woman? Oh! And did I mention she is a dream?"

Looking exasperated, and tired from a night of tossing and turning, Simone suddenly, and to her horror, sensed her eyes welling up.

"Oh, Monie, I'm sorry. I didn't mean to upset you. Jeez!" Maggie said as she reached out and took Simone's hand. Simone readily grabbed Maggie's and squeezed it.

Shaking her head, she wiped her eyes before any tears could fall. "No, it's okay. It's not you. It's well, I'm trying to process what's happening, but it simply doesn't make sense. I mean we live in the twenty-first century; this isn't a fairytale." Looking up to the sky, she sighed heavily, "Ever since I walked into that shop in Florida, Metamorphosis, my life has not been the same. Meeting Henry, finding the jacket that couldn't possibly have belonged to Amelia Earhart, the dreams of the beautiful woman, and now, the trunk

81

and its contents." Suddenly releasing Maggie's hand, Simone looked spooked. "Mags...you don't think I'm going crazy, do you?" she asked in earnest.

"No, don't even go there. I've seen the trunk, remember? I've seen the photos and I believe you. We just need to figure this out."

Suddenly remembering Annie's dream, Simone quickly updated Maggie on what Annie had shared. "Wow! Who knew there was actually something to all those dreams Annie has had since she got whacked on the head by that flowerpot?" Laughing slightly, Maggie added, "I guess we should stop teasing her, huh?"

Smiling, Simone said, "Well maybe...nah, not so much," Both women laughed. After agreeing to call Maggie in the next day or two, Simone walked home through the park. Her thoughts were consumed with everything that had happened over the past month, the abrupt end to her engagement, the dreams of the blond woman, Henry, the trunk, the photos that had shocked her into the realization that her dreams were leading her to something. Something, ...but what? God, I hope I'm not losing my mind!

*   *   *

An orchestra played a soulful jazz tune; the horns, smooth and deep, filled the room. Simone smiled at the enchanting stranger whose beautiful face sparkled with amusement. She knew her own smile must be broad and telling, but she didn't care. She was so happy to see this magnificent woman again.

Reaching out her slender hand, the woman smiled expectantly and confidently. With butterflies swarming in her stomach, Simone laid her hand in the woman's outreached palm and was led out onto the dance floor. As the woman guided Simone with a gentle touch to her lower back, she spoke, but Simone couldn't hear her over the sound of the music. Watching her soft pale lips, she struggled to make out her words. Was she introducing herself? Yes, she heard her say her name, Vivian Oliver.

Looking closely at the woman as they moved slowly to the music, Simone was mesmerized; she felt as if this woman could see into her soul. Their mutual attraction was palpable, and her heart soared. "I'm Simone...Simone Adan and I am so happy to meet you."

Simone woke with a start and sat up in bed, breathing heavily. She rubbed her temples and groaned. Hopping out of bed, she paced her carpeted bedroom floor. She was flushed from her dream. The intense feelings of seeing this woman and being in her presence made her head spin and her heart race. She walked to her living room and pulled open her balcony doors. Stepping out onto the balcony, she sat down hard on her loveseat. "Vivian, please, please be real," she said.

After sitting outside for the better part of an hour, Simone felt chilled. Rubbing her hands together, she padded barefoot into her living room and sat in front of the trunk. Taking a deep breath, she reached over and slowly opened the buckles of the leather straps. Removing the open padlock, she held it in her hand for a moment, noticing for the first time that it was solid brass. It shined as if it was brand-new. It was heavy and well-made, almost as if it were crafted by hand. Raising her eyebrows, she realized it might have been. Slowly turning it over, she read the letters engraved into the metal on the bottom. "V.T.O.," Simone whispered, "Vivian, Vivian Oliver."

As she opened the trunk, she focused on the photos pinned to the inside lid. "Vivian, you are so beautiful," she said, smiling. "I see you are also an adventurer with all these places you've traveled to." She gently touched a few of the photos as she scrutinized each for clues as to who Vivian could possibly be.

Looking closely at the interior of the trunk, she was impressed by the many compartments and small to medium-sized drawers it contained. It was beautifully made, most likely handcrafted by a skilled craftsman. Every space was utilized as the compartments had been created to make use of the entirety of the trunk's interior. This was a trunk for long travels to faraway places she concluded.

When she and Maggie had initially opened the trunk, they never made it past the photos and eyeing its gleaming interior with its many compartments of various sizes. This was mostly due to the shock of identifying Vivian as the woman who frequented her dreams. They had talked as they looked at the photos for what felt like hours. At one point, Simone had taken one of the dresses, folded neatly in tissue paper, out of the trunk and she and Maggie had carefully examined it. There were no labels, and the stitching was beautifully and expertly done, leading them to conclude that the garment was made exclusively for the owner of the trunk.

Maggie wanted to begin going through each compartment immediately but, feeling that a certain sense of respect was due to this amazing woman, Simone had convinced Maggie that this was something she needed to do alone. Maggie had reluctantly agreed, knowing how important this was to her friend, but she had made Simone promise to update her immediately once she had completed her investigation.

Now, alone, Simone felt the time was right to continue looking at the contents. Despite this trunk now being her property, she was surprised that she continued to feel some reluctance. She almost felt like an intruder, sorting through possessions that had been the cherished property of another. Biting her lip, she told herself she was acting silly. Henry had said, "Enjoy the journey." She felt certain that this trunk was part of her journey.

*   *   *

Reaching for her cell, she saw that it was nearly 5:00 p.m. Stretching, she rubbed her tired eyes. She had been slowly and meticulously going through the contents of the trunk for hours. Each compartment, each drawer that she opened, made her heartbeat faster with excitement and anticipation. It was as if she had opened a treasure chest from history and discovered the amazing life of Vivian Therese Oliver. She had learned, from journals she had found in one compartment, that Vivian was a scientist, an anthropologist, and an educator. Simone smiled at the thought. "I knew you would be amazing," she said.

Simone had discovered that Vivian had lived in New York in 1923 where she was a Professor of Anthropology, specializing in the indigenous cultures of southern and eastern Africa. Reading through her notes and journal entries gave Simone a sense of who Vivian was. Her words jumped off the page; her excitement at new discoveries, as well as her solemn self-reflection on disappointments, gave Simone insight into Vivian. There were personal observations on the beauty of the places she visited, concerns for the earth and its populations that inhabited these beautiful lands, and detailed references to the people she had encountered. Shocked, but with a knowing smile, Simone found a photo of Vivian, pressed between the pages of one of her journals. She immediately recognized the other women in the picture. Vivian was standing with a fellow adventurer named Amelia Earhart. They were both smiling, their hair blowing in the wind. The back of the photo simply read Amy and Viv, 1920, Columbia University. Simone looked closely at the photo. One could see they were intimate, perhaps best friends. "Holy shit," Simone said quietly, "Amelia and Vivian. Perhaps, Amelia, you were impatient for me to open the trunk. That's the reason you gave me the key." Shaking her head, she placed the photo back between the pages.

With each careful reading of a journal, each intimate observation of a photograph, Simone felt a growing closeness evolving between Vivian and her. It was as if they were somehow connected. It was a heady intoxicating feeling. Despite her excitement, she was apprehensive as to what could possibly come next. She had no idea.

After placing all items carefully back in the trunk, she gently closed the lid. Sitting back, she smiled. "What an amazing woman you are Vivian," she whispered. She had decided that the trunk, filled with writings, books, tools, and work clothes, as well as a few gowns, jewelry, and personal items, must have been bound for a long journey, most likely aboard a ship. The trunk, with all its contents, had never made it to Vivian and, over the next hundred years, had somehow found its way, unscathed and intact, to Henry's unusual shop.

A thought occurred to her suddenly and she sat up abruptly. Is it possible that she has a history? Of course, she must! Walking quickly to her home office, she sat at her desk, booted up her laptop, and waited. "Okay," she said as she typed in a Google search. Feeling a bit apprehensive, she hesitated to hit the Enter key. What if she were married, or had a longtime partner, or…or, worst of all, what if she didn't exist? "Stop!" she said. "Stop, get a grip! There's a purpose for us connecting." Taking a long breath, she willed herself to relax. Hitting the key, she closed her eyes; when she slowly opened them, she saw several Vivian Olivers on the screen. But none was her Vivian. Braving another search, she typed in Vivian Oliver, anthropologist. Nothing. Then she tried Vivian Oliver, 1923. There was nothing, absolutely nothing. "Okay," she said, taking a moment to calm herself. "Think. Yes! The photo of Vivian and Amelia at Columbia University." Typing in Columbia University faculty, she caught her breath when she found a reference in their archive to a Professor Vivian Oliver who, for a short time, had been a visiting faculty member. There wasn't much, a few words specific to her credentials and time spent there, but it was her. It was her Vivian; she was certain of it. Leaning back in her chair, she breathed a sigh of relief. "You do exist; I knew you must."

*   *   *

Her tea was hot, with a hint of spice. It soothed her and warmed her hands as she held tightly to the cup. Sitting on her balcony to catch the last bit of sunlight, she continued to contemplate the woman she has come to know as Vivian Oliver. Vivian had existed; she had found proof, a short reference in a university archive, yes, but she was real. Sighing, she accepted the truth; she was falling in love with her, this woman who did not live in her world but who moved freely through her dreams. "Who are you, where do you come from? Well, whoever you are," she whispered, "I know in my heart that our destiny is connected, I just know it." She was certain that meeting Henry and finding the trunk were not random. She believed that everything that had occurred over the past weeks was meant to bring her to this moment of realization, and ultimately, to Vivian.

CHAPTER 9

Autumn, 1923

"Professor Oliver," Dr. Escabar said in an annoyed drone, "we need you over at the dig site. It seems one of our students requires your assistance identifying some unusual artifacts." Looking up from her lunch, Vivian responded kindly. Despite her disdain of Escabar, she believed that, in the best interest of the expedition, professional courtesy was warranted. As she prepared her equipment for the walk to the dig site, Dr. Handler approached.

"It's difficult, isn't it?"

"What's difficult?" Vivian asked. He led her out of earshot of the others and continued.

"To keep from cringing when he speaks. He is appalling and, once this dig has ended, I intend to report his behavior, though honestly, I don't hold out much hope for any investigation or reprimand. Escabar is world-renowned. Financers of expensive and lucrative expeditions tend to overlook such behavior when huge budgets are involved and there is potential for significant prestige for a museum and our university."

Sighing, Vivian looked at him and she nodded her agreement. "Honestly, David, I can barely tolerate the sound of his voice. I anticipate an unpleasant working environment ahead if what we witnessed yesterday is an example of his behavior." David nodded as they both looked in the direction of the dig site. "Well," Vivian said, "we'd best get to it. History awaits!" With that, they made their way to the site.

As the workday progressed, the temperature grew stifling. Despite the heat, the team had managed to make some excellent progress during their long hours in the sun. Vivian knew it would take the better part of a week to clean and identify the many pieces of pottery, metal, and bone, and then catalog and preserve them. These were exciting finds and she looked forward to getting to work.

The late afternoon sounds of the vast Kenyan landscape began to make themselves known as Vivian walked the familiar path back to camp. Insects, birds, and small creatures scurried about with each step she took. The heat, sticky and thick, left her feeling as if her work boots were made of lead. Wiping her brow, she looked up at the sky. Evening was approaching and with it, a reprieve from the scorching sun. Deciding to take a short detour, she removed her boots and socks and dug her toes in the soft earth as she walked to the water's edge.

Lake Victoria was magnificent; the setting sun was reflected on its glass-like surface. Allowing the cool water to soothe her tired feet, she sighed in contentment. Hearing the laughter of children, she turned toward the sound to witness a glorious sight. Several children, their beautiful dark skin glistening in the setting sun, laughed and played in the cool water. It looked inviting and it was all she could do not to jump in with them. Instead, she pulled her camera from her bag and snapped a few photos. Smiling, she couldn't wait to develop them and add them to her collection. Thinking now, she sighed heavily, realizing that several of her very favorite photos were pinned to the inside lid of her missing trunk. "Where in the world can it be?" she whispered. Not only were her favorite photos in the trunk, but also a few well-loved pieces of her grandmother's jewelry, as well as a few of her journals that she had brought along to review in her downtime. She had hoped to consolidate much of the details from her dig experiences into a draft of her academic paper. The draft would be the first step toward her next publishing effort. Walking back toward camp, she squared her shoulders and resolved to let the lost trunk go. She could certainly draft her paper without her notes, plus everything here at the Kenya dig was more than enough to publish.

"Vivian. Come, I have prepared a cool bath for you." Snapping out of her internal musings, Vivian looked up to see a very thoughtful face.

"Oh, Amidah," Vivian said, startled. She was shocked to see that she had made it back to camp. Looking around, she huffed out a small laugh. She had been so caught up in her thoughts that she hadn't paid attention to where she was walking. "Thank you, you are very kind," she said as she gently touched Amidah's arm. "You do know that this is not necessary. I don't wish to give you more chores. You work hard enough without catering to me."

Laughing lightly, Amidah shook her head. "It is no burden, child, I have time. I have also left you a meal in your tent. You must eat to maintain your strength." Smiling now, Vivian acknowledged Amidah's kindness and walked toward her tent to gather her bath supplies.

*   *   *

"Oh, excuse me, I hadn't realized anyone else was in here. I can wait until you've finished, Professor." Turning to leave the bath tent, Vivian halted mid-step when she heard Professor Smith speak.

"Please, call me Mary Elizabeth, and, as we are both women, I see no need for you to leave," she said, gesturing to the full canvas tub. "I see that Amidah has prepared your bath. I don't wish to interrupt. I am nearly finished." Smiling, Vivian nodded, though, if truth be told, disrobing in front of a near-stranger made her terribly uncomfortable unless they were about to be intimate. Blushing slightly at the thought, Vivian cleared her throat and slowly began to undress.

"Vivian, our Amidah seems to have taken quite a liking to you," Mary Elizabeth smiled. "You are fortunate as she is quite revered in her village. Many of the workers here stop and lower their heads when she passes. It's quite astonishing. I myself feel very honored to have her respect." Vivian stopped disrobing and turned toward her companion.

"She *is* quite amazing, isn't she?" added Vivian. "Escabar said something about her being a…healer."

Mary Elizabeth laughed heartily. "You know very well that horse's ass called her a witch doctor. He should take heed, I dare say. I'd not be in any hurry to make an enemy of her." Vivian laughed lightly at Mary Elizabeth's colorful description of Escabar.

"I agree with you," Vivian said as she again started to disrobe for her bath. "He makes my skin crawl. I am doing my best to ignore his arrogance, as well as his obvious disdain for me. His cruelty is appalling. If I ever see anything like what he did to that poor girl again, I'm reporting him immediately. Thank goodness for David's quick intervention. Ugh, I cringe when I think about how he put his hand on my lower back when we first met." She squirmed at the memory.

Mary Elizabeth looked appalled. "What? No, don't tell me. I'm sure it was entirely inappropriate. He fancies himself a ladies' man. I have been here for several weeks now; the way he glares at the young women from the village is inexcusable. He has exhausted me to no end with his contempt for the indigenous community and his utter disrespect for their practices and traditions. Honestly, he shouldn't be too quick to dismiss their beliefs. However, the fact that he does is not surprising." Turning now to Vivian, Mary Elizabeth said, "You do realize that Amidah is a powerful Laibon? It is my understanding that she is the only female Laibon amongst the Maasai people. Her healing, divination, and prophetic abilities are quite legendary."

Stepping into the cool water, Vivian turned toward Mary Elizabeth. "What? Amidah is a Laibon?" Vivian said incredulously. "My God, it's no wonder," she said as she sank into her bath, "that when I'm with her I feel as if I am in the presence of someone powerful."

As Vivian settled in the tub, Mary Elizabeth looked thoughtful. "Vivian, she is powerful. I can feel it in my bones," she whispered, almost in reverence. "Good lord, that woman is formidable. Only Escabar is foolish enough not to see it." Heaving out a sigh, Mary Elizabeth grabbed her towel and toiletries. Turning to Vivian, she smiled, "Until tomorrow, Professor Oliver."

Smiling back, Vivian gave a quick salute as she sank into the cool bath. "Until tomorrow."

Lying now on her cot, clean and cool, Vivian closed her eyes and listened. She could hear the sounds of the night, the trees rustling in the gentle wind, the faraway sounds of animals calling to one another, and the rhythmic movement of Lake Victoria. She thought about the next day's plans. She would rise early, have a quick breakfast, and spend another full day at the dig site. She was good with that. This is what she needed, she told herself, a structure, a focused routine to help her get back to herself.

She was uncomfortably aware that she'd not been fully vested in meeting her goal of publishing again. Her previous published work had been very successful, but it had been a few years back. She needed to publish another paper to remain a viable candidate for tenure.

As a key member of the expedition, she would have significant material to publish in her field, based on her research and findings. This was her perfect opportunity and she needed to seize it. If she were ever to secure the coveted tenured professorship at the University of Chicago she so wanted, she had to move forward. Her father's alma mater had always been her dream. She believed she was ready. She was growing tired of her own wanderings and craved more, not so much success, but the fulfillment of a goal.

Months ago, she had admitted to herself that she was afraid, afraid she'd fail and tarnish her celebrated father's name. Up until quite recently, she wasn't ready to meet her fear head-on so, instead of facing it, she had made excuses and ignored any opportunity that could move her toward her goal. She had gone from woman to woman and party to party, telling herself she had plenty of time to get serious. Yes, she had been teaching and that was her joy. But one day she awoke with a pounding head, in a bed with a woman whose name she couldn't remember. She felt terrible for the woman and ashamed of herself. She knew then that she needed to step up and not be afraid to take the bull by the horns. It was time to grow up. The chance to participate in the Kenya expedition was a godsend. When the Dean at the university had called her into his office and offered her the opportunity, she jumped at it. This was her chance to contribute her expertise, to prove to herself that she was her parents' daughter.

Smiling now, she remembered her wonderful parents who had both perished in a shipwreck off the coast of South America three years earlier. The pain of their loss ran deep; she missed them tremendously and loved them fiercely. They had always supported and encouraged her, and now it was her turn. She would be the woman they always believed her to be.

Vivian took a drink of champagne; the bubbles tickled her nose, and the cool crisp liquid sliding down her throat felt wonderful in the stuffy confines of the ballroom. She longed to go out to the garden where the air was cool and fresh. Placing her glass on a tray, she turned to walk toward the open doors when a slow jazzy Bessie Smith tune began. She smiled, and turning toward the sound, caught her breath…it was her, the beautiful woman of her dreams, standing near the orchestra. She held her breath for a moment and could not stop the smile that slowly appeared on her face. She watched as the woman spoke with a handsome man who appeared mesmerized by her. Then, as if Vivian had called to her, she turned, and their eyes met. Her smile was mesmerizing, warm, and sensuous.

Vivian found herself walking toward her, and, as if it were the most natural thing in the world, she reached out her hand and invited the woman to dance. When the woman nodded and placed her hand in Vivian's, the sensation was magical. Placing her other hand on the small of her back, Vivian led her out onto the dance floor. "My name is Vivian Oliver," she said, "I am so very pleased to finally meet you." The woman looked at her questioningly. Vivian realized she couldn't hear her over the music of the orchestra. But then, she watched her mouth as her soft rose-colored lips whispered Vivian's name. She smiled broadly and said, "I am Simone, Simone Adan, and it's my pleasure."

Sitting up abruptly, she tumbled off her small cot and onto the floor of the tent. "Simone, your name is Simone," she smiled and whispered aloud, "What a lovely name…Simone Adan."

"Professor Vivian? Are you alright?"

Vivian looked up toward the alarmed voice only to see Amidah standing at the entrance to the tent with a look of surprised concern on her face. Vivian quickly realized it was early morning. Amidah must be making her regular morning rounds bringing fresh water and towels. "Oh! Amidah…yes, I am perfectly fine," she said embarrassedly. "A dream, I had the most realistic dream," she said, almost to herself, "I must have woken with a start. Nothing to worry about, I'm quite fine, thank you."

As Vivian untangled herself, she watched Amidah slowly walk into the tent shaking her head. Vivian watched a smile form on her lips as she slowly made her way to the camp desk to set out the water and towels. Blushing, yet smiling she said, "Amidah, are you laughing at me?"

Turning back, Amidah's wide grin exposed one very large dimple on her chin, making her smile all that more infectious. "Why yes, I am," she said, without a bit of pretense or regret, which only made Vivian laugh out loud. "You know, dreams are very telling. They can be the window to our true destiny." Shrugging her shoulders, she continued, "Or they can simply be dreams. It is up to the dreamer of dreams to determine what is true, and what is simply…a dream."

Vivian stared at Amidah for a long moment. "Amidah," Vivian said, worrying her lip with her teeth, "Professor Smith shared with me that you are a Laibon." Turning once again to Vivian, Amidah looked at her; her expression was filled with a knowledge and understanding that Vivian could not even hope to comprehend. After several long moments, Amidah slowly made her way toward the open flap of the tent entrance. Vivian was disappointed that Amidah was not going to respond.

Without turning, Amidah stopped as she pulled back the tent flap to leave. "I was born the only child of our village's Laibon, destined, after the death of my father, to be their guide. It is an honor and a burden." Turning now, she smiled at Vivian. "You will find your path; your journey has only just begun."

"Wait!" Realizing she raised her voice, Vivian blushed. "Oh, I'm sorry. Please, can you stay a few moments? Here, sit…please," she said, gesturing to her camp chair. Amidah looked closely at Vivian and, after a moment, nodded, sat down, folded her hands, and laid them gently in her lap. She said nothing but simply watched as Vivian gathered her thoughts. Sitting on her cot, Vivian rubbed her forehead. It was several moments before she spoke. "Amidah…I, I have been having dreams. They seem so real," she said quietly. Looking at Amidah, she repeated her words, "So very real."

Amidah closed her eyes slowly and seemed to have fallen asleep. Disappointment flowed through her again. She wanted Amidah to tell her some truth to help her to understand why she was having dreams of a woman whom she had never met. What did it mean? She desperately wanted to understand, and she wanted to believe that the woman from her dreams was much more than her imagination.

While her mind spun with questions and a growing need to find answers, Amidah breathed in deeply and then spoke. "We are in an age of infinite wisdom, yet human beings have not yet evolved." Looking at Vivian, she continued, "We are like the aged turtle, we can live long, but we hide our heads in fear and close our eyes to all possibilities, except what we can touch. In doing so, we do not see what is before our eyes."

Looking toward Amidah, Vivian did not speak. She waited breathlessly. As if tired from a long hard day, Amidah slowly stood. "Humanity believes in a finite world, yet we are ever flowing, we are ever moving, evolving, and changing. We focus so much on what is now that we do not see what is beyond our own reality. We look to the stars and believe we are the center of the cosmos; we are not. There is so much more, so much that can be possible, if only we would be open to seeing beyond our own realities."

Moving from her bed, Vivian stood. Turning to Amidah she spoke with conviction. "I *believe* Amidah...I mean, I know what finite is; I am a scientist. However, I also know there is more, much more. These dreams I am experiencing, they're more than my imagination. I feel it, I believe it." Looking at Amidah with eager excitement, Vivian's shoulders suddenly slumped as she realized that she sounded desperate. She sighed and said, "Will you help me? Will you help me on my journey?"

"We have already begun. Lie down, my child." Vivian did what she was told. She stretched out on her cot and laid there quietly with her eyes closed. She sensed Amidah standing over her. She could feel light moisture drip slowly down past her eyes to the side of her face; she dared not wipe it away. Her hands shook as they lay tightly against her sides and, as her lids fluttered open and then close once again, she felt an energy—a thick, vibrating energy—engulf her. It began at her forehead and then slowly, like a warm blanket, covered her entire body. She kept her eyes closed. Her eyelids were heavy, and she felt a deep lethargy overtake her. She did not want to sleep. It is not what she expected nor wanted but she simply could not keep herself from drifting into slumber. As she slipped deeper, she felt a sudden shock, as if she were traveling on an elevator spiraling upward. Eyelids fluttering, she saw glimpses of time pass, a dance of hours, days, and years. Suddenly, as if a blaring alarm alerted her, she sat up with a start.

A light cool breeze engulfed her, and she wrapped her arms around herself. She was standing on a balcony; she wobbled slightly at the sudden shock of it. It was one she had never seen before, small but lovely with colorful plants sporadically placed throughout and a petite comfortable-looking lounge that was situated to offer a view. The view itself was unbelievable. It was a city at night, but none that she could have ever comprehended. It was lit with a million lights. Enormously tall buildings stood like monuments to some eternal god, and, beyond the city, there was an enormous waterway, an ocean or perhaps a sea; she didn't know which. She had no clue where she was, nor how she got there. She wasn't even certain she was awake; her dreams tended to be so real these past weeks that it was difficult to know for certain. Turning slowly, she felt the soft touch of fabric, a drape she realized after a start, a drape, moving slowly in the breeze, had grazed her hand.

Turning toward an open door, she heard a quiet intake of breath and stared, stunned, as Simone stood in the doorway looking around. She slowly walked backward but realized Simone couldn't see her even though she stood only a short distance away. She believed that Simone could sense that there was someone else there, on the balcony. It was the look on her face; a look not of fear, but of wonder.

Vivian watched her and smiled with the poignancy of seeing this beautiful familiar face that she had dreamed of so often. She wanted to reach out to her and take her hand and say, "I'm here. Simone. It's me, Vivian." She moved forward toward the door and, standing within inches of Simone, she reached for her hand but found that she was unable to grasp it. As much as she tried, only wisps of light traveled from her outreached palm to Simone's. "Simone," she whispered, as she watched Simone's gentle eyes widen with an acknowledgment that filled her with hope and warmth.

*　　*　　*

Eyes fluttering open, she felt an intense pain in a small corner of her temple. Placing a trembling hand over her face, she moaned. Nausea suddenly overtook her; she turned quickly to empty her stomach. Leaning over the side of her cot, she retched into a bucket that she'd never seen before. Once done, she immediately felt better. Sitting up slowly, she saw it was no longer early morning. The heat of mid-day was intense, and the sun shone too brightly into her tent, intensifying the pain in her head. Amidah was quietly sitting next to her, moving to soothe her forehead with a cool rag. A sudden feeling of loss overtook her and a sadness she hadn't expected overcame her. "Simone," she whispered. Tears slid from her eyes, and her heart felt tight. The sight of Simone, the woman from her dreams with her sweet face and gentle smile, had touched her soul. "Amidah," she whispered pleading, "Please, I must find her."

CHAPTER 10

Holding her breath and focusing on the door leading to the balcony, Simone stood very still. An overpowering, unmistakable sense of another's presence sent her body into full attention mode. She wasn't afraid. She knew instinctively that it was Vivian who had found her way to her somehow; she was certain of it. Reaching out hesitantly, she gently pushed aside the curtain and very slowly stepped out of the door. Her eyes made their way around her small balcony. As she scanned the area, she could feel her heart beating intensely. A fierce feeling of excitement and longing coursed through her. "Vivian, my dream woman," she whispered. Smiling to herself, she felt suddenly silly thinking of Vivian as her dream woman. Yet that is what she was to her, and she had a deepening desire to know her. She felt there was a connection that was strong and intimate.

Now, as the lights of the city sparkled and the soft breeze of the evening brushed her skin, she waited breathlessly, for what she wasn't certain. Before she could have another thought, she felt a touch, light and faint, against her hand. The gentleness caressed her, and her heart swelled with the sweetness of it. She knew without a doubt that it was her. The feel of the light pressure disappeared as quickly as it appeared and she almost cried out at the loss. Leaning against the glass door, she put her arms around herself, and, at that exact moment, she heard her name whispered softly with the same longing she herself felt. "Oh, Vivian, it is you? I know it must be. Please come back."

*   *   *

"I believe you, Simone, I do," Annie said as she sat at her desk in her office and watched her sister pace the small room.

"I know how this all sounds," Simone said as she stopped her frantic pacing and plopped down into a chair. Head in her hands, she took a deep breath. "I don't understand how this is possible, but it's happening. I have met a woman, who I believe is from the past, and quite possibly another earth, who is somehow reaching out to me." Lifting her head, she stared at her sister. "Annie," she said, almost afraid, "You don't think she's a spirit? Oh, God, please don't let her be a spirit."

"Simone, you're a smart woman. You know that we, here in our world, cannot be the only beings in existence. There are other planes of consciousness, other dimensions, other worlds that we, as humans, cannot even begin to comprehend. Merely because we cannot see or touch them does not mean they don't exist. We cannot simply assume, because we don't understand, that other levels of consciousness can *only be attributed* to spirits." Looking at her sister, Annie grabbed her hand, "I believe you. I believe that you and this woman, this Vivian, are meant to know each other, that there is indeed a connection. I promise I will help you in any way that I can."

Relaxing, Simone leaned forward. "I…I can't stop thinking about her. I fall asleep praying that she'll be there in my dreams.

But yesterday…it wasn't a dream, I'm sure of it. I don't even know how to explain what it was, but it wasn't a dream. She really was there, in my home."

*   *   *

"Slow down, Simone, I can't keep up!" Maggie gasped. Simone turned and saw that Maggie was a good ten yards behind her. They had gone on a morning run that had started out routinely enough. However, as Simone focused on the previous day's discussion with Annie, and what she had experienced a few days earlier on the balcony of her condo, she had become completely distracted. She had not even realized that they were well past their usual stopping point.

Quickly halting her run, she bent over and put her hands on her knees, "Oh, Maggie, I'm sorry," she said between breaths. "I'm not focused this morning."

"I think you're focused, it's just not on our run. Come on, let's head back to your place and you can cook me breakfast while you tell me about yesterday's conversation with Annie."

Looking at Maggie, Simone shrugged, "Okay, it's the least I could do after nearly running you to exhaustion."

"What did Annie say?" Maggie asked. The two friends were in Simone's kitchen drinking coffee while Simone chopped onions for scrambled eggs. Simone had shared with Maggie that she was certain that Vivian had somehow been here in her home and, more specifically, on her balcony.

Simone sighed. "She said a lot of things. Clearly, I have not been paying attention to how knowledgeable Annie has become concerning alternative theories of life beyond our own physical existence. I have to say, she has impressed the hell out of me. She has given me a lot to consider. For one thing, she said that it is very possible that Vivian is real and that she is reaching out to me through some alternate space or dimension, and that the trunk, the trunk may be the catalyst. I know it sounds crazy, but what Annie is saying…well, it makes sense. I mean, for one thing, the dreams only began after I discovered the trunk at Metamorphosis. Then, there was the mystery of how I found the key." Running her fingers through her hair, Simone sighed heavily. "I don't know, Maggie. Annie believes that Vivian will try to reach out to me again, that she is trying to connect with me." Looking at Maggie, she smiled sadly, "I really hope she is. I can't explain it, I only know that I feel a connection with her, and I need to know her."

"Wow!"

Simone looked up from her chopping, "Wow what?" She waited for Maggie to continue.

"Wow, you got it bad. It appears you're in love with her. Are you?"

Looking at Maggie, Simone put down her knife and wiped her hands on a towel. Maggie waited. "I feel such an incredible connection with her that, at times, overwhelms me. I think of her constantly. When I wake up each morning, she is the first thing on my mind. During the day, I want to know what she's doing, where she is…and at night, before I close my eyes, she's the last thing I think of before I fall asleep. Am I in love with her? Yes, it seems that I am."

*   *   *

Vivian felt a cool breeze tousle her hair and make its way through her khaki shirt. Goosebumps sprang up on her forearms as she slowly turned her head to scan her surroundings. She was back on the balcony of Simone's apartment. She wanted to scream, both in elation and fear. Amidah had done it; she had helped her return! Though this time, she felt whole. She believed, no she knew, that she was physically present, in Simone's world. Amidah had said to be fully present, one must believe, and she did believe. She believed with her whole heart that Simone meant her future. She desperately wanted to see her again, to connect with her this time and let her know that she was real and not a figment of her imagination.

Huffing out a short laugh she looked down at herself, realizing she was dressed as she was when Adamah asked her to lie down, in khaki shorts, a white shirt, and work boots. It was not the best outfit to impress a lady. Walking the short distance to the glass door separating the balcony from Simone's living space, Vivian checked the latch; it was unlocked. She slowly slid the door open. Just as she was about to step into the room, she heard the sound of a key in a door. Vivian took in a quick breath. Moving quietly but swiftly, she crouched down and hid herself behind a large planter that separated the balcony from Simone's living room. Panic made its way through her; she could feel her heart beating a mile a minute.

She took a deep breath to help steady her nerves and told herself that this is what she wanted; there was no need to be afraid. Yet, despite her internal pep talk, Vivian was worried that she would frighten Simone with her sudden appearance. After all, it wasn't as if she lived in the same time period. Hell, she wasn't even sure they lived in the same world. Peaking ever so slightly around the planter, she quickly covered her mouth to stop her gasp. It was her, Simone. She was dressed simply, in a crisp aqua shirt with the collar up, and tight, black, form-fitting trousers made from some sort of stretchy material. If this is how women dressed in Simone's time, she thought, she'd like it here very much. "Concentrate," she said. Suddenly, Vivian saw Simone pause and put down her brief-case. She was looking around, moving slowly, eyeing the room, "Okay, she knows someone is here, it's now or never," she whis-pered. Just when she was about to come out from behind the planter, she heard Simone speak.

"Okay, whoever is here, come out now!" Vivian saw that Simone had picked up a poker from the fireplace and was holding it like a weapon. "I'm a blackbelt in Tao Kwan Do. I will beat you with this poker, then I will break your face with my hands if you don't show yourself. Now, come out!"

Vivian had no choice but to show herself. This wasn't the way she wanted to meet the woman of her dreams, but she knew she had no choice. "Don't! Please…uh…I can explain!" Vivian ap-peared from behind the planter, hands stretched out as if ready to stop an attack. Her breath came in deep gasps as she stared at the beautiful woman before her.

Simone felt, rather than heard, herself scream when she saw Vivian stand up and take a step toward the living room. Staring unbelievingly, the poker slipped from her hands, landing with a thud only a few inches from her feet. "Oh, good lord! Is this really happening? It's…it's you! But it can't be, but it is. How is this pos-sible!?"

In the time it took for Simone to process that Vivian Oliver was real and standing in her living room, she had already decided that she was so much more beautiful in person than in her photos. Even standing there with arms out to protect herself, hair in a wild, messy bun, and wearing strange khaki clothes, she looked glorious.

"Oh! I've scared you half to death! Please forgive me. This is absolutely not how I wanted to introduce myself. You must believe me!" cried Vivian. Watching Simone continue to stare, apparently speechless, Vivian quickly determined that she must explain herself as best and as quickly as possible. "Please, may I come in? My name is Vivian Oliver…ah…I will explain everything, if only you will give me a chance."

Simone couldn't stop staring. Vivian Oliver stood in front of her, flesh and bone, not a dream but a beautiful woman, a very real woman. "It's really you, but how?" Realizing that Vivian was waiting for her to invite her in, she quickly led her into the living room.

Slowly and carefully making her way into Simone's living space, Vivian felt her heart pounding and willed herself to relax. She watched as Simone slowly backed up, giving her a wide berth. She couldn't blame her; she probably would have done the same thing if their circumstances were reversed.

"May I sit, please?" she said, quietly gesturing to a comfortable-looking chair near the balcony door. "I'm feeling a bit out of breath and, to be honest, rather spooked at the moment." Simone nodded her approval slowly. Vivian breathed a deep sigh as she sank into the soft comfort of the chair. Looking up at Simone from her seated position, who stood wide-eyed, incredulous, and absolutely adorable, in Vivian's opinion, she couldn't help but let out a small laugh of relief. Seeing Simone's shoulders immediately relax at the sound of her laughter, and watching a beautiful smile crease her face, confirmed that coming to Simone's world was the exact right thing to do.

Simone felt an instantaneous sense of release hearing Vivian's soft laughter. To her, it was a beautiful telling sound, a sound of incredible relief and joy. It wasn't a mistake, she realized. Vivian wanted to be here; she was certain of it. She sensed that Vivian wasn't afraid or regretful. Continuing to look at her, Simone slowly made her way to the couch across from where Vivian sat. There, she seated herself crossed-legged on it just as she had as a child. "I can't believe this, Vivian Oliver, here." Blushing, she said, "I'm sorry, I sound like a ten-year-old child in awe of her favorite action hero. It's just so incredible that you are here. I'm still trying to process it."

"Simone, no need to apologize; I feel the same," Vivian gently offered. After a moment of uncomfortable silence between the two women, Vivian began. She spoke of her vivid dreams of the two of them over the past weeks. Simone listened closely. Vivian's voice, Simone noted, was soft, but with an assuredness that she could not help but admire. Vivian explained how she came to know Simone's name, and how, in her dreams, they had met at a ball and had shared a dance. Was that a blush on Vivian's cheeks, Simone wondered? Vivian's description of Amidah, a powerful seer who had guided her to where she now found herself, rang true to Simone. Vivian spoke of how Amidah had helped her to realize that there are no finite realities, that many journeys were possible. She shared her belief that being physically present, in Simone's world, could not possibly be an isolated occurrence. She was certain that it had been the experience of others and, most likely, would continue to be in the future. Finally, with an assurance that gave Simone hope, Vivian quietly said that she was certain that Simone was a prominent part of her unusual journey, and she believed that they shared a strong connection. Hearing Vivian's words gave Simone the validation that she longed for, that their meeting was meant to be, that it was not simply a bump in the cosmic universe.

When Vivian suddenly stopped speaking, Simone was surprised, so intently was she listening. Sitting back, she allowed Vivian's story to sink in. She noted curiosity in Vivian's gaze as she waited for Simone to speak, and she could feel a slight apprehension from her that was neither ominous nor dangerous. Simone felt no danger from this woman. On the contrary, she felt comfortable and immensely happy to have Vivian here in her world.

"Vivian Oliver," she said softly, as she looked at the slightly disheveled woman who sat across from her. "Thank you for sharing your story with me. I am Simone Adan, and I am so pleased to meet you, in person, at last. This is all so incredible," she said, smiling and shaking her head in wonder. Vivian let out another small laugh and nodded in agreement. "Um, okay," Simone said as she moved to sit closer to Vivian. "I...I want to share what I know as well." Looking at Simone, Vivian waited.

As her nervous hands moved through her hair, she settled herself and looked directly at Vivian, "Where do I start?" she said, still in a kind of mild shock at seeing this amazing woman sitting here, in her home. She had no clue how to begin. She stood up suddenly and began slowly pacing. Finally, she shook out her hands and turned, only to see Vivian waiting, patient and attentive. "I was in Florida," she began, "with my fiancé." Seeing Vivian's surprised expression, she immediately clarified. "My ex-fiancé, I am not...engaged to anyone, not at all." Clearing her throat, she continued. "We were visiting his family. Uh...more specifically his mother, to get her approval...you see." Vivian was looking at her, appearing slightly confused. "Okay...okay. Sorry, that's not important. I had gone shopping with Katherine, that's her name, my former fiancé's mother. Anyway, we had gone to a consignment shop, and I was bored, so I went outside the shop to wait. Oh, hell, this is not going well, is it?"

Simone closed her eyes. Giving herself a moment, she opened them slowly, took a deep breath, and said, "Okay...I was having a coffee when a little man came out of an unusual shop called Metamorphosis. I helped him with a planter...anyway, I went into the shop, and it was lovely and strange and unique. That is where I found what couldn't possibly be Amelia Earhart's jacket, and music boxes that played in sync and where I saw your trunk. It caught my attention immediately. It was just what I had been searching for; it was perfect. Anyway, now here it sits." She waved her hand toward the trunk, a vase of violets resting upon it.

Vivian's gaze followed Simone's movements and she gasped, suddenly realizing that she was staring at her trunk, her missing trunk. Her mind reeled as she stood slowly and moved to gently touch the familiar leather straps. Her trunk, here…in Simone's world. "Good heavens," she said quietly. "Is this it…is this our connection? Of course, it must be! How in the world did my trunk make its way here?" Putting her hand to her forehead, she tried to think. Then, a realization hit her with a force that nearly made her stumble. She had no idea where she was. She must be in America …but where? And more to the point, when? When was she in America?

"Are you alright?" Simone asked, concerned now as Vivian looked about to pass out. "Please sit, before you faint."

Ignoring the statement, Vivian said, "How…why is it here, in your home?" Pacing now, she turned to Simone. "Simone, please, tell me something that will help me to understand how this is all possible and that you are real," she said, almost frightened, "and not a figment of my imagination and that I have not completely lost my mind."

Simone was at a loss for words. How could she explain something that she herself did not understand? She believed that there was a real reason for their meeting, that, despite time and space, they were meant to know each other. But how could she say that without sounding ridiculous? She desperately wanted to know Vivian, and she definitely did not want to frighten her. She had to be honest, just as Vivian had been with her.

"Vivian, I wish I had answers to share, but honestly, I have no idea how this, us coming into each other's lives, is possible. However," she said with conviction, "I can assure you, I am most definitely real."

Admiring Simone's resolve, Vivian stood, momentarily watching her, then sat back down. Clearing her throat, she spoke. "Simone, have you had dreams? Have you had dreams of you and I meeting?"

"Yes!" Simone said, with an elevated voice that she thought sounded a little bit too much like her mother. Lowering her voice to its normal range, she continued. "Since I purchased the trunk, I have dreamed of you, …of us, very often. Then, a few evenings ago, I could have sworn you were here, on the balcony. Were you here, Vivian?"

"I was," Vivian said, suddenly feeling tired and in need of something strong to drink. "I was out there," she said as she pointed to Simone's balcony. "However, I felt almost like a spirit. I mean, as if I were between two worlds. Perhaps that is what occurs when one doesn't fully transition." Lifting her head, she smiled softly, "Though I know that I am truly here now." Tapping the arm of the chair as confirmation, she looked at Simone. "Yes, truly physically here. Um, Simone?" she said, now looking a bit sheepish. "You wouldn't happen to have any Scotch, would you?"

A tender smile made its way across Simone's lips and she felt a sudden lessening of her own nervousness. "You're in luck," she said gently, "I happen to enjoy Scotch whiskey on occasion, and I believe we both can use it right about now. I'll be right back." Walking into the kitchen, she leaned against the kitchen island, straightening her shoulders as she worked to calm her frantic heart. She needed to pull herself together. Finding the Scotch, she poured two fingers for each of them, took a deep breath, released it, and made her way back into the living room.

After handing Vivian her drink, she lifted her glass in a gesture of a toast and watched as Vivian drank the strong liquid down in one quick movement. Following suit, she quickly downed hers as well. The pungent taste of the Scotch made its way down her throat and created a slow burn in her belly. Savoring the feel, she stood quiet. It was a few moments before she spoke. "That was nice. Can we start again?" she said quietly. She saw Vivian's lips draw into a soft smile as she nodded.

"I think that you know quite a bit more about me...and who I am...than I know of you. Tell me, how do you...know about me?" Vivian asked shyly.

"The trunk. It was your trunk and its contents that introduced the real you to me." Leaning back, Simone folded her legs under her in a relaxed pose, giving Vivian her full attention before she spoke again. "As I walked through this strange little shop, I saw your trunk displayed in a small alcove. A beam of light from a window gave it an almost majestic appearance, like a king's chest filled with riches. I loved it, Vivian. I was fascinated by its unusual and intricate details and the silver buckles and soft leather straps. The stickers from the various ports fascinated me; I felt certain they were authentic. I knew that this beautiful trunk must have an amazing history and story to tell. It wasn't until I tried to lift it, while examining its details, that I realized it wasn't empty. When I asked Henry what was inside and if he could open it, he said that I must purchase the trunk as is, *that those were the rules*. I thought it strange of course, but he was so earnest. The entire shop was magical, Vivian. I had no choice but to buy it; my heart insisted."

Vivian listened intently, rapt with curiosity and awe at hearing Simone's story. She could not help but feel a connection with Simone, not just the Simone of her dreams, but the real woman, the lovely wide-eyed creature seated across from her. She needed to know more about Simone, she wanted to know more. "Tell me Simone…tell me about you."

Simone couldn't stop herself from grinning, not teasingly, but with hope at the soft way that Vivian spoke. She felt a sudden relaxed acceptance from Vivian, an almost playful challenge, curious and thoughtful.

CHAPTER 11

Waking slowly, Vivian smelled the rich aroma of coffee brewing and squinted at the bright sun beaming through Simone's billowy soft curtains. She felt warm and snug on Simone's comfortable couch under a soft, downy, dark orange coverlet. Yawning, she sat up and eyed Simone as she moved about in her small kitchen. She smiled, thinking that Simone looked lovely in a blue patterned silk robe as she prepared their coffee. She felt her heart constrict as she watched her sway happily to soft music coming from some contraption situated on the kitchen counter. She smiled at Simone's easy joy and thought of their long discussion that had lasted deep into the night.

Simone had explained, in detail, the story of Henry and his strange little shop that had seemed to come from out of nowhere. She talked of exploring the trunk's contents and how she felt almost an intruder for doing so. She spoke of Michael, and her dear friend Maggie, and her sister Annie. In turn, Vivian shared the story of her parents and her dream of becoming a full professor at, of all places, the University of Chicago, which was Simone's alma mater, as well as Vivian's father's. They both spoke without pretense and in an easy way, much as if they had known each other for ages, but with the added excitement of something entirely new.

In one beautiful evening, Vivian had learned more about Simone than she had ever cared to know about any of her other friendships. More surprisingly, she had shared more about herself than she had ever shared with anyone else. It was refreshing and freeing, and she had no regrets. Still, the shock of hearing that Simone lived in Chicago one hundred years in her future took some time to absorb. It wasn't until Simone shared some of the history of the world's last hundred years and had shown Vivian a few of the modern devices that Vivian understood the magnitude of her situation. Still, as she sat watching Simone, it took all her concentration and knowledge of Amidah's skills to fully comprehend where and *when* she was sitting.

"Since I didn't know how you take your coffee, I brought out a variety of sweeteners and creamers. I like mine milky and sweet, but I don't think that's the norm for most people." Simone said as she walked into the living room. Biting her lip, she told herself to stop blathering. She knew she was nervous and, as soon as she opened her mouth, babble fell out. Handing Vivian a cup of coffee, she thanked the powers that be that her hands didn't shake and expose her nervousness. She could barely keep her eyes off her, the beautiful woman with tousled blond hair sitting crossed-legged on her couch. They had talked deep into the night and, as it grew late, neither wanted to end the evening. As Vivian had nowhere else to stay, Simone insisted she spend the night. She had suggested that, by morning, things would be a bit less daunting. Now, as she sat across from Vivian in the full light of day, everything felt very daunting. One thing was certain, Simone wanted to know her; she wanted to know everything about Vivian Oliver. She couldn't help herself.

"Simone?"

"Yes?"

"What are these small packets used for?" Simone looked down at the various sweeteners she had laid out on the tray and realized Vivian would have no clue what they were.

"Oh! Sorry, I should explain." Reaching over she pointed to the various sweeteners. "Okay, this little brown packet is raw cane sugar, the pink is Saccharine. You really don't want to use that, it tastes awful. The blue is called Equal, and the yellow, Splenda. Oh, and this cup here holds almond milk," she said, pointing to one of the small containers, "and this is nonfat milk and the other is non-dairy creamer." Looking up at Vivian, she couldn't help but chuckle at the bemused look on her face.

"My word! All this for a simple cup of coffee?" Vivian laughed.

"It does seem ridiculous now that you point it out. So, how do you take your coffee?" Simone asked, laughing quietly as she prepared her own cup.

"Black," Vivian said, smiling at Simone as she lifted her steaming cup to her lips.

*   *   *

She was gone. Simone had gone to fetch more coffee and, when she returned not a minute later, Vivian was no longer there. Her nearly empty cup still sat on the trunk; the decorative pillow she had been leaning against as they spoke still held the indentation of her form. Her aura still lingered in the room but she was gone. Simone scanned the room, then quickly walked to the balcony hoping she had walked out for a breath of air, but there was no sign of her. She had disappeared as inexplicably as she had appeared. Plopping down on her couch, Simone felt dazed, trying to comprehend what had just happened. Running her fingers through her hair, she was startled by the sound of her ringing cell. "Maggie…hi. No, I'm fine. I just…you're here, now? Okay, yes come up. I'll buzz you in."

Opening the door and seeing Maggie standing there with sudden concern evident on her face nearly made Simone burst into tears. "Simone? What's the matter? You look devastated." Turning away, Simone walked back into the room, letting Maggie make her own way into the condo.

"Would you like a coffee? I have an entire pot ready to pour. I also made muffins this morning, raisin walnut." Grabbing a cup out of the cabinet she misjudged her grip and the cup crashed to the floor. "Fuck!" Before she could reach for the broom, Maggie reached for her arm.

"Monie?"

"Oh, Maggie!" Simone's eyes filled with tears and her hands trembled.

"Monie, sit, please." Taking Simone's hand, Maggie led her to a stool at the kitchen island, grabbed two cups, and poured them each a coffee. "Now, please tell me what has happened."

Leaning forward, Simone put her head in her hands. What could she say? Could she say that a woman from a hundred years in the past had come to visit her and that they were having coffee one minute and the next she was gone? Sitting up, she looked at her friend. If anyone would believe her, she knew it would be Maggie. Resigning herself to telling the truth she began. "She was here, Maggie. Vivian Oliver was here. She slept on the couch, and we were having coffee…and then I walked away just for a moment. I went to the kitchen to get us a refill and, when I came back, not one minute later, she was gone. Now I don't know if she will return."

Maggie looked stunned. "Your Vivian Oliver was here? Here in your condo? Are you serious? Yes, I mean ...I know you're serious but, what the fuck!" Realizing she wasn't helping the situation with her outburst, she quickly reached for Simone's hands. "Oh, shit, I'm sorry. I didn't mean to freak out. It's just so shocking. Okay, okay, let me try and process this. I need a second." Looking around the room, she turned back to Simone. "How? I mean, how did she get here, when did she get here? And where is she? Where is she now?"

"I don't know!" Simone cried, exasperated. "I don't know where she went." Simone hugged herself and slowly walked over to the couch and flopped down. "Yes, it's crazy, it's unbelievable, impossible even! I know this is how it seems, but it happened."

Quickly making her way to Simone, Maggie knelt in front of her and reached for her hands. Giving them a squeeze, she held them tight. Sighing deeply, Simone managed a soft smile and then stood. Maggie watched as she walked to her cabinet, grabbed a glass, and poured water from the tap. After drinking down half the glass, she looked at Maggie and walked back into the living room. She then began to tell Maggie how Vivian had simply appeared on her balcony the previous evening, how she was so shocked to see her that she had been struck speechless with wonder and confusion. Then, she shared with her Vivian's story of the African woman who helped to guide her to Simone's world.

"Maggie? Have I lost my mind?" she said softly, feeling suddenly drained. Turning, she pointed at the couch that Vivian had been sitting on. "She sat right there on the couch, and now, now she's gone." She touched the back of the couch, remembering Vivian's smile, and her shoulders slumped in sadness.

"I really wish I had the right words to comfort you." Walking over, Maggie turned Simone so that she was facing her. "But I will tell you that I believe Vivian being here was not random. I believe that her presence in your life is meant to happen. Everything that has happened since you returned from Florida means something important to each of you. This can't be the end, Simone, there is no way. I believe you will see Vivian again."

"Oh, Maggie, I do hope you're right." Eyes welling with sudden tears, she felt Maggie's warm soothing embrace. She held tight thinking of the woman who held her heart.

*   *   *

Vivian woke with a start, stomach churning with the now-familiar feeling of nausea, she turned quickly to vomit into a bucket by the side of her cot. "Shit! Shit! Shit!" she muttered as she wiped her mouth with a rag that was suddenly thrust at her. Sitting up slowly, she looked right into the amused face of Amidah.

"Welcome back, Professor Vivian. How was your journey?"

Pale and drenched in sweat, Vivian stared at Amidah, remnants of the nausea she had just experienced lingering slightly. "Jesus, Amidah!" Vivian breathed as she reached for the glass of water that sat on her side table. With trembling hands, she thirstily drank down the entire glass before turning once more to Amidah. "Amidah…she's real. Truly real." Stretching out her hand she slowly closed her fist and spoke softly. "I touched her. She stood in front of me, lovely and kind…in an impossible world with strange gadgets, sparkling lights, and ten different ways to drink coffee."

Amidah looked deep into Vivian's eyes and smiled gently. Then, as if she floated on air, she rose from her seat and made her way out of Vivian's tent. "Yes, you are as real to her world, as she is to yours. You must decide. Vivian. You must decide soon."

"I…I don't understand," Vivian whispered as she watched Amidah move the tent flap back to exit.

"Our windows to other worlds close, often…unexpectedly. It is the rare soul who perceives her future as assuredly as you have been given the opportunity to do, to physically move through time and space and exist in a world that you were not born into. You must decide."

*　　*　　*

It had been nearly three days since Vivian awoke back in her tent and had listened to Amidah's cryptic words. She desperately needed answers. "You must decide," Amidah had said.

Today, the sun was shining through the tent opening and the heat made her skin sticky with sweat. Rubbing her eyes, she tried to focus. It was nearly 7:00 a.m. She should be at the dig by now. She knew Escabar would be livid. Facing his wrath was not something she wanted to deal with, but she knew it was inevitable.

"Professor Oliver? Sorry to disturb you, but you are wanted at the dig site, ma'am."

"Yes, I'll be there shortly," she responded through the closed flap of her tent. It was one of the student researchers; she didn't know which one, but she was sure that Escabar had sent him to check on her. "Lord, I despise him," she whispered to herself. She had witnessed him browbeat nearly all the researchers, even going so far as to try and reprimand senior members of the team.

Since the incident that first morning when she and David had stopped him from striking the young woman, he had been short-tempered and demanding and, for some reason, he seemed to be especially confrontational with her. She was certain it wasn't her imagination. According to Mary Elizabeth, he hated women being on what he perceived to be *his* expeditions. However, she felt there was more to his disdain for her than her being a woman. It was how he continuously questioned her findings and always insisted on seeing her field notes. Was he trying to catch her making a gross error, thus attempting to discredit her? Whatever he was trying to do, it unnerved her. Taking a moment, she breathed deeply. It's okay. I will not allow him to intimidate me; he is simply a bully with a big ego. Once this expedition is finalized, I will never need to see him again. Until that time, I know I'd best tread lightly.

Walking to the dig site, she felt tired and edgy. The heat was already oppressive, and it was still very early. As she trekked along the familiar path, she thought of Simone. She had not dreamt of her for two nights now. It concerned her and, if the truth be told, she missed her terribly. Since their encounter, she had thought of nothing but their time together. Those hours they had shared had been wonderful. Smiling, she said, "Well, once we calmed down and were no longer terrified of each other, our time together was amazing." She felt an intense connection with Simone, and she was certain Simone felt that same connection with her. She wanted to know what Simone was thinking right at this moment. Was she thinking of her? She was certain that Simone would have been distraught once she had returned from her kitchen to find that she had vanished. It was all making her crazy! Simply disappearing like she had. She didn't understand it, she needed to see Amidah. She would know how to get her back to Simone. She had to return to her, but she hadn't seen Amidah in two days, and her inquiries as to her whereabouts had generated no answers.

As Vivian had expected, Escabar was in a foul mood and glared at her with such disdain that it was almost comical. The only time he acknowledged her was when he was reprimanding her. He had practically screamed at her, insisting that she had held up nearly an entire morning's work with her tardiness. Now, as the sun was setting and the work for the day was coming to an end, she only wanted to get back to her tent and lie down. She was exhausted and could still not stop her thoughts from returning once again to Simone. Slowly following the shoreline back to camp, she thought of Simone's smile. Lost in her thoughts, she nearly missed seeing Mary Elizabeth, standing next to her tent smoking a cigarette and looking agitated. "Mary Elizabeth, hello. How are you this evening?"

Taking one final puff, Mary Elizabeth dropped her cigarette and ground it out under her boot. "Vivian, can we talk?" Vivian looked at her curiously and nodded. Mary Elizabeth took her arm and entwined it with her own, leading them both slowly back toward the shore. "Let's walk," she said as she put her finger to her lips to stop Vivian from speaking. Once out of earshot of the campsite, she lit another cigarette and smiled at Vivian.

"I think, Professor, you and I…shall I say, have some commonalities. I won't mince words as I am nothing if not direct. I recognized you immediately from that lovely women's soiree in London last fall. You had a charming companion with you as I recall." Vivian felt the heat of a deep blush run through her body at Mary Elizabeth's words. She did indeed remember that evening, as her date for the evening would not stop kissing her neck.

Smiling at Vivian's blush, she continued. "Our taste in sexual partners is not why I have come to speak with you. Though," she said, with a hint of amusement, "while I do think that our common interest in the feminine persuasion could be a rather fun discussion, I shall save that topic for another time. Right now, well, I suppose this is my way of assuring you that you can trust me and know that I am sincere." Vivian stopped walking; looking directly at Mary Elizabeth, she waited.

"Vivian, there is talk around camp that Escabar is out for blood. He cannot be trusted. You must be cautious. David and I overheard him discussing your work with some of the team. We did not like the direction he was taking the discussion. He sounded as if he was attempting to convince anyone within earshot that you had stolen his ideas. We can't help but believe he may be attempting to shanghai your findings and pawn them off as his own."

Vivian was about to speak when Mary Elizabeth put up her hand to stop her. "Look, I have read your articles and have an inordinate interest in your findings and theories. I am a great admirer of your work and I've no doubt that it is *your work*. I simply want to warn you to be cautious and alert. Escabar has maneuvered his way into many respected societies and is a master of manipulation."

"You can't be serious! Why in the world would he want to steal my work, or anyone else's for that matter? I don't understand any of this. Tell me, what am I missing here?"

"I am warning you, Professor, you must be cautious. There was an incident a few years ago where he sued a group of anthropologists out of Edinburgh. He had worked with the team briefly a few years prior and he claimed that an article they published was actually his work. He asserted that they stole his notes from his apartment. It was ridiculous, of course, and eventually, it was settled out of court. However, Escabar won a judgment, and then had the audacity to take their work and rewrite it in his own words and publish it. Those poor blokes didn't have a chance; Escabar is that conniving. David and I believe he is now setting the stage to try and pull something just as diabolical. I don't know what, I am simply advising you to be cautious."

"Mary Elizabeth," Vivian said, astounded. "Are you certain?" She disliked Escabar immensely but had never considered the possibility that he would plot to steal her work. "This is insane. Who is this man anyway? How can he be so highly regarded in the field if what you are telling me is true? I know that I have felt his immediate dislike for me, however, I never considered he'd go so far as to…"

"I promise you, what I am telling you is true. I have worked with other scientists who know Escabar's reputation for doing this kind of thing. Don't put anything past him. He is a man, already given more respect and rights simply for being born with a penis. He is also the son of a highly regarded forensic anthropologist who, before he died, made certain that his son followed in his footsteps. Now, I do not know much about his father, but what I do know is that he was brilliant and evidently demanded complete loyalty from those in his circle. Rumor has it that he was not a pleasant man." She looked at Vivian, "Apparently the apple didn't fall far from the tree." Taking a deep drag of her cigarette, she blew the smoke out, creating a sweet-smelling haze.

"Look, I knew when I first arrived that working with him would be a challenge. He is not keen on women being smarter or more accomplished than he sees himself. However, I have experience with him, so I was prepared. Whatever you do, do not allow him to read your notes. Send them off by courier to the university immediately. Try to send them before he has an opportunity to ask you for them. He actually does have a right to view them since he is the head of the expedition, but I would not put it past him to ask for them to read privately. I don't trust him, and you shouldn't either. As long as you keep aware, he won't have an opportunity to try anything sinister."

Mary Elizabeth looked at Vivian and smiled. "Oh, don't look so stricken. If you keep on your toes, he won't be able to best you. You are an intelligent woman, I've no doubt you can handle any attempts he makes to take credit for your work." Walking away, Mary Elizabeth turned back, smiled, and tilted her head. "My lovely

Mazie would like you. Anyway, I must be off. I have a few letters to write. Cheerio, Professor."

Vivian watched as Mary Elizabeth walked back toward her own quarters. Considering everything that was shared, Vivian did not doubt Mary Elizabeth's sincerity, nor did she consider ignoring her warning. She decided then and there to contact the university by telegraph and courier regarding her final write-up, once it was complete. She knew it would take weeks to arrive, however at least it would be safe and out of Escabar's reach. She would also let them know that she would be returning to the States as soon as possible. Her work was nearly complete; she and her team had finalized the cataloging of all artifacts. She was also secure in knowing that her paper, all sixty-five pages of it, would be well received by the university and museum. She had documented a very compelling theory on how the ancient people of this village had lived and died. She was immensely grateful to her team and to both Mary Elizabeth and David for their expertise and assistance. The idea of Escabar stealing her work and claiming it as his own emboldened her to be more aware of his every move. She knew she must take Mary Elizabeth's warning seriously.

As she walked back toward her own tent, her head spun with what she had just learned. Still, this new information had not distracted her from her goal of speaking with Amidah. She had to know how to contact Simone. She wasn't leaving until she could see Simone again and tell her…tell her what? What could she tell her, that she was falling in love with her? Tell her that there had to be a way for them to be together? Shaking her head, she realized it all sounded impossible. She felt exhausted and she needed to sleep. She would have a clearer head in the morning and would search out Amidah then.

Opening the flap of her tent, pitch darkness hit her. Too tired to light her camp lamp, she laid down on her cot. "Simone," she whispered as her eyelids closed. Sitting comfortably across from her in the small camp tent, Amidah smiled and folded her hands onto her lap.

"Vivian?" A soft excited smile graced Simone's face as she reached out and touched Vivian's cheek. "Vivian I...I think we're dreaming," said Simone. "Quickly, I must tell you...I was heartsick when you disappeared. We hadn't had enough time. There is so much more for us, so much I want to share with you. I want to be with you Vivian, no one else, only you." Not being able to stop the broad smile that crossed her own lips, Vivian reached for Simone's hand. Half expecting her fingers to move through air, she was shocked to feel the warm softness of Simone's skin.

"I've missed you, Simone," Vivian whispered, as if speaking too loudly would wake them from their fragile sleep. Looking deeply into Simone's eyes, she moved to close the small gap between them. Lifting her head, she pressed her lips to Simone's. The exquisite softness of her mouth made her swoon and desire shot through her. She could feel Simone respond in kind.

Opening her eyes, she felt breathless with disappointment. She was lying on her cot in her tent. "A dream," she said.

"Yes, a dream, but a lovely one, was it not?" Vivian abruptly sat up on her cot and looked to the corner of the tent where Amidah sat quietly, hands folded, eyes closed. "A dream with immense possibilities. You, my child, are the rare soul that can move between worlds. There are many worlds, do not doubt that as fact. However, we as human beings, as do other beings from other worlds, go through our lives not knowing that our private space is not private at all, but occupied by those only a mere dimension away." Amidah lifted her arm and, like a maestro conducting a symphony, moved her hand slowly through the expanse of space.

Hearing Amidah's soft voice and cryptic words, Vivian felt dizzy with both relief and trepidation. "Amidah..." she said softly.

* * *

A chilly wind made her teeth chatter. Shuddering, she put her arms around herself. She was freezing; the thin field shirt she wore was pathetically inadequate for the cold wind that whipped through this strange city. Scanning her surroundings, she saw bright lights and heard the faint sounds of traffic. "I'm here...I'm back." She smiled gratefully. Amidah had done it. She had helped her return, just as she said she would. A feeling of both excitement and apprehension seized her as she could hardly wait to see Simone again. Turning quickly to make her way toward the living space, she saw a stunned Simone standing near the open balcony door.

Staring at each other, it took a few moments for them to actually acknowledge that they were both there, together. They said each other's names at the exact same time. Simone quickly stepped forward. Reaching for Vivian's arm, she guided her into the warmth of her cozy living room. Gripping her hand, she gently moved Vivian to the couch. Vivian allowed the touch without resistance. Grabbing a throw, Simone gently wrapped the warm blanket around Vivian's shoulders and then, kneeling in front of her, she rubbed her arms to help warm her.

"Simone...I...I've come back to you," Vivian said, blushing at her own words. Hearing Simone laugh sweetly, she herself laughed at her own joy.

"Yes, I can see that," Simone whispered as she continued to gently rub the chill from Vivian's arms.

"I...I had to see you again. I wish I could explain what's happening, however, I don't entirely understand it myself. All I do know for certain is that seeing you here and not in a dream is, well, everything." Vivian said breathlessly.

Reaching up slowly, Simone gently brushed whisps of blond hair off Vivian's face. That gentle sweet gesture lit a small fire in Vivian's belly. Reaching for Simone, she leaned into her warm embrace. Then, as in her dreams, their lips met gently; the feel of soft sweet pressure was what she knew it would be, tantalizing and exciting. A breathy moan escaped her as Vivian guided her tongue to glide into Simone's open mouth. "Oh, God," she whispered. She could feel her heart rate escalate. She heard a soft whimper from Simone and felt strong arms gently enfold her.

Completely surrendering to Simone's touch, she allowed herself to be swept away by this beautiful woman. As their kiss deepened, so did her feelings. She couldn't believe how Simone made her feel; every part of her was on fire. She wanted nothing more than to know her, to be with her, to devour her. She knew, without a doubt, that she loved Simone and that she was *in* love with her. Lifting her hands, she gently cupped Simone's cheeks and slowly pulled away from their kiss. "You are so beautiful. I am just over the moon to be here with you in your world." Leaning in once again, she moaned when she felt the pressure of Simone's arms around her. Moving her body closer, the softness of their breasts touching sent a tantalizing shock from her heart to her groin. Slowly, she lowered Simone onto her back and moved herself so that she was cradling her in her arms as they explored each other's mouths.

No other woman had ever made her feel this way; every nerve ending in her body sparked, she felt on fire. She could feel the pounding of her heart and Simone's in tandem. Moving her mouth down to taste the warmth of Simone's neck, she could hear herself whisper words of adoration. This was so much more than pure desire, this was love. Goosebumps rose on Simone's soft skin as Vivian kissed the hollow of her throat; moving slowly down she nipped and sucked tenderly. As Simone's excitement grew, Vivian felt emboldened and moved to her breasts. "Sweet Jesus," she whispered. The feel and touch of Simone was exquisite, soft and subtle, yet strong. Overwhelmed, she spoke. "Simone, please, I need you."

With that declaration, Simone lifted Vivian gently off the couch and led her to the bedroom, where they collapsed onto the bed and, without hesitation, removed their clothing. As Vivian disrobed, her excitement seemed to overwhelm her, but it was the understated movements of Simone, slow, enticing, and sensuous, that truly gave her pause and ignited her senses. Their lovemaking that night was powerful, exciting, and gentle. They explored each other's bodies without inhibitions and instinctively sensed what the other enjoyed sexually. They forged a bond that was cemented with each touch, each kiss, and when they held each other closely as they climaxed, they knew they could never be apart. They had found their destiny in each other.

CHAPTER 12

Waking just before dawn, Simone yawned. Soft light shone through the windows and the sun was just beginning to peek over the horizon. Turning her head slightly, she dared a glance to see if the remarkable woman that she spent the night with remained in her bed. Breathing out a grateful sigh, she smiled as she watched her sleep peacefully beside her. Vivian Oliver, scientist extraordinaire, explorer, world traveler, and now lover, lay next to her in nothing but soft glowing skin. Blowing out a breath and leaning back on the pillow, she closed her eyes. "Vivian Oliver, here," she whispered, "finally here...with me."

Turning onto her side, she reached out and gently moved a wayward curl from Vivian's smooth forehead. The tenderness overwhelmed her. "This glorious woman," she whispered, "how can we be together?" Covering her eyes with her arm, she closed them and reassured herself that they could figure this out...we can, and we will. Suddenly, a gentle hand touched her cheek; it was warm and soft, and the tenderness of the gesture touched her heart.

"What are you thinking my darling?" Vivian rolled over and Simone had to catch her breath. She was so beautiful. The sheet covering Vivian's back slipped and revealed soft strong shoulders and sleek toned arms.

"Come here," Simone said softly as she reached over and pulled Vivian into her arms. Immediately she felt the tug of her excitement. Nothing had ever felt so good, so right. Kissing Vivian deeply, she basked in the feel of her. As she moved her knee up and over Vivian's lower body, she heard the enticing sounds of Vivian's breath catching, escalating in quick bursts of excitement. Kissing her way down Vivian's throat, she gently massaged her breasts and slowly moved her mouth to suck and tease her nipples that had grown taut with want. Had she ever tasted anything so wonderful? She couldn't recall. Vivian's gasps and words of love simply were going to push her to orgasm on their own. She'd never been this turned on. Now, moving her hand down to between Vivian's legs, she gently guided them open.

She could feel Vivian, wet with need; gently circling her soft folds, she slowly inserted one and then two fingers, curling them just as she had done last night. However, this time she moved her body slowly and lovingly downward so that her face was within inches of Vivian's moist sex. Gently lifting Vivian's leg over her shoulder, she moved to taste the exquisiteness of this woman.

"Ohhh!" Simone moaned at the first wonderful taste of her and every nerve ending in her body screamed her desire. Now, moving her tongue to match Vivian's excited thrusts, she reached down to touch her own wetness and a sharp jolt of excitement ripped through her. She could feel both of their orgasms building. Vivian's hands held her shoulders tightly as she moved her body in rhythm to the movement of Simone's mouth. Suddenly, she felt a sharp tug of her hair at the scalp and could feel Vivian's legs go taut. A low, long, deeply satisfied moan followed as Vivian's orgasm erupted. Seconds later, Simone plunged her fingers deep inside herself, and the strongest orgasm she had ever experienced ripped through her. "Oh, God, Vivian…oh, baby…Fuck! Ohhhhhh!"

*   *   *

Simone swallowed her tea and smiled as she watched Vivian, sitting cross-legged on the couch, marveling at the magic of her iPhone. Grinning, she thought about how she had spent a good part of the morning explaining what she knew of the technology and how it operated. Vivian was awestruck and simply could not wrap her considerably brilliant brain around the concept. Simone had decided then and there to ease Vivian into the marvels of the twenty-first century so it would not overwhelm her. Moving from her chair to the couch, she scooted close, charmed by Vivian's wide-eyed stare and looks of astonishment as she stared at the small screen. She was watching a particularly energetic music video of Camila Cabello, doing her hit "Havana." Simone could not help her amusement as she leaned in to watch the video with her. "So, tell me, Ms. Oliver, how do you feel about the advances of the past one hundred years?" Looking at Vivian with a genuine smile, she waited for her to respond.

Turning to look at Simone, Vivian simply shook her head. "I don't understand it. To me, it is magic…a science fiction tale that is make-believe. Yet, I can see that it's all entirely possible." Putting her hand to her forehead, she paused. "I think I could use another cup of that extremely strong tea that you brew."

"Coming right up," Simone said as she reached over to Vivian and gave her a sweet gentle kiss which produced a soft sigh from Vivian and a dazzling smile. "Okay…be right back." Practically skipping to the kitchen, she realized that she never felt happier. This was it. All her life she had known that there would be that special someone who she'd want to spend her life with; she had simply never considered it could be a woman from another time and place. Yet here she was, in the flesh.

Walking back into the living room with two mugs of steaming hot tea, her heart sank. Setting the tray of hot beverages down, she moved to the couch. Smoothing out the indentation of Vivian's body, she sat down. She was gone. She knew it as surely as she knew now that she absolutely loved her. She was gone. "I hate this!" she yelled. "Oh, Vivian, please come back, I don't want to be without you anymore. I love you."

*   *   *

"Oh, hell!" Deep rasping gasps tore from Vivian's throat as she leaned over her cot and vomited into the bucket that sat next to her bed. She felt lightheaded and overheated as she breathed in large gulps of air. Grabbing a cloth from the side table, she mopped her perspiring neck and face. She was back in her tent and no longer with Simone. The realization nearly broke her heart. A sob of frustration escaped her; she covered her mouth to quiet the sound.

"Professor Vivian, the pain in your heart does not need to be…you have the power to change it."

"Amidah!" Sitting up quickly, Vivian stared in the dark toward Amidah's voice. "How is this happening?! Good heavens…this is all so impossible! I've left her, I've left her again!" Sobbing softly, she covered her face with her hands. "Please, what must I do? I need to be with her. Can you help me…please?" Falling back on the cot, Vivian worked to control her emotions. She took several deep breaths and exhaled slowly. After a moment, she spoke, "Forgive me, I will pull myself together. Please, just give me just a moment."

Looking around, she realized that it was evening. The last thing she recalled was morning coffee with Simone. "Have I been gone long? Last I remember, it was early morning, and…and I was with Simone."

Shrugging her shoulders, Amidah spoke, "You have been away only as long as you have been away. Time in parallel worlds can be years or decades apart. However, minutes and hours do not always follow suit. It is a mystery. However, it is the nature of how it is."

Vivian watched Amidah briefly. Then, moving from her cot, she stood and slowly began to pace. As she adjusted to the darkness, she turned and saw the silhouette of Amidah's face, with its soft wisdom dominating her profile. A sort of aura surrounded her and Vivian felt a growing strength and clarity from that aura. A feeling of calm quietly embraced her and the uncertainty of only moments ago vanished. "Amidah," she said clearing her throat, "I believe that I have been given an amazing gift, an opportunity to change the direction of my life if I so wish." Feeling exhausted, she could not stifle a yawn. "However, for some reason, at this moment I cannot seem to keep my eyes open, I'm suddenly so tired." Moving back to her bed, she sat and felt herself drifting off.

In the darkness of the small tent, Amidah folded her hands and closed her eyes. "Sleep now, Vivian, sleep and dream."

Hearing the curtains dancing in the soft breeze, and smelling the scent of Simone's perfume, Vivian awoke. Yawning, she looked up. "Well sleepyhead, you're awake. Good, I was beginning to feel neglected." A teasing Simone sat down on the lounger that Vivian lay in and handed her a lemonade. "Here you go beautiful, a cool drink for a hot lady." Simone laughed at her own silly joke. "Sorry, that was pretty corny, but you're beautiful and your mussed and tousled look is just too adorable to ignore."

"Simone? Simone, you're here. I mean, I'm here!" Sitting up, Vivian took the glass and placed it on the small table next to her lounger. "Come here,

please." With that, Vivian pulled Simone in for a searing kiss. "Oh, darling, I am so happy to see you," Vivian whispered in Simone's ear as she skimmed her dark hair with her lips, "I thought I'd lost you again."

Pulling back, Simone appeared contemplative to Vivian. Her face was thoughtful and a bit sad. "Vivian, my love. This isn't reality, baby. We're dreaming…but what a beautiful reality it can be," she whispered.

Feeling a sudden stifling heat, she sat up. Simone was no longer there, with her. Alone in her tent, she fell back on her pillow and sighed.

* * *

Making her way to the mess tent, Vivian was in dire need of a strong cup of coffee. The late morning sun was already high and the heat was oppressive. She had slept badly, and the dream of Simone only gave her more to think about.

"Professor Oliver! One moment, please." Vivian had just made her way into the tent, which was teeming with activity, when she heard the irritatingly shrill voice of Dr. Escabar. Turning, she nearly ran into him. "You were not present at this morning's dig meeting," he hissed. "Please explain yourself, Professor. This is inexcusable! Really, Professor," he said with a leer while his eyes took in her whole body, "your beauty sleep has caused the loss of valuable time, or is it your menstrual cycle that is interfering with your ability to work?"

Vivian's temper ignited but, instead of taking the bait, she sighed deeply and silently calmed herself. She was aware of his obvious efforts to rile her up, but she refused to play into his hand. She knew that everyone was waiting to hear how she would respond. She had to be cautious. It was obvious to her that he was creating a scene for the purpose of fortifying his authority in front of the others. However, today she was prepared and was most definitely not bowing to his brutish bullying.

Turning to face Escabar, she shifted her gaze and noted that every person in the tent was watching the two of them with anticipation. She felt that her response to his tirade would surely cement both Escabar's and her reputation amongst the team. She despised this role-playing tightrope. Over the past weeks, she had rarely defended herself against his innuendos and nasty remarks. She foolishly believed that not responding would tire him out and he'd give up on attempting to rile her. She had even, on one occasion, stood by quietly while he treated others as if they were present only to serve him. However, now, well now she had had enough. She could not allow him to believe he could speak to her, or anyone else, in the demeaning way he just had.

"Dr. Escabar, good morning," Vivian said in an achingly calm voice. Stepping a foot or so away from him so that he no longer stood in her personal space, she looked directly at him before she spoke again. "First, I find your tone and words to be highly inappropriate and insulting. I would even go so far as to consider them threatening. Are you threatening me, Doctor? Because if you are, I will find it necessary to report you immediately to our superiors."

Looking at Vivian, Escabar's nostrils flared. Vivian could see that he was working hard to hold in his anger, however there was no way she was going to back down. She wanted the team to see that his bullying would not be tolerated.

"Secondly, Doctor, I do not, nor have I ever, reported to you. I am your colleague and, as such, have no obligation to respond to your unfounded criticisms. However, as we have an audience," Vivian said, looking around the tent, "I feel compelled to update the team on the status of my findings and final analysis."

Turning to face her colleagues, she spoke, "Team, I am very

excited to share with you that we are far ahead of schedule. From the copious bone fragments and artifacts that you have excavated over the past several weeks, I have been able to piece together a hypothesis regarding the time period for the community that occupied this terrain. I have also conferred with both Professor Smith and Dr. Handler and they have provided their enthusiastic approval regarding my hypothesis' clarity and probable accuracy. With their input, and with the documentation complete, I feel secure in couriering our final report to the university and the head of the museum sponsoring our expedition. You have all been extremely supportive and the work could not have been completed without your dedication and expertise. Thank you and congratulations."

An enthusiastic gasp and words of praise and approval filtered throughout the space. Turning, she responded with genuine appreciation to her colleagues and fellow team members as several patted her on the back and reached to shake her hand. Jumping slightly at the sound of a loud bang, she turned in time to see Dr. Escabar pound the table that held the coffee. The vibration of his meaty fist sent the cups and coffee pot flying. No one moved. Looking at Escabar now, Vivian felt real concern at the color of his face; he was flaming red. He appeared to be in the midst of a serious heart attack. Several of the team tried to come to his aid, however he brushed them off and stormed out of the tent.

"Professor Oliver?" Turning, Vivian saw David Handler and Mary Elizabeth Smith approaching.

"David, Mary Elizabeth, hi. I didn't see you two earlier. Were you present for that fiasco?"

"Oh, yes," responded Mary Elizabeth excitedly. "Damn, Viv, you handled that splendidly. I thought for sure that horse's ass was going to blow a gasket!"

Turning to Mary Elizabeth, Vivian puffed out her cheeks and blew out a sigh. "Seriously, thank you for the vote of confidence. I could not allow him the satisfaction of believing that he could get away with speaking to me or anyone else that way. Horse's ass indeed!"

*   *   *

The shade felt glorious, such an unexpected gift on an especially hot and sticky day. It was early afternoon and, since the team had taken the afternoon off for some much-needed downtime, she took advantage of the opportunity and made her way to a spot on the beach that she had discovered. It was secluded and a bit off the beaten path so she could think clearly and peacefully without being disturbed.

Squinting, she looked out toward the water. Whitecaps crashed against the jagged rocks that were peppered along the shore. A warm breeze whipped through her hair, blowing sun-bleached strands across her eyes that she impatiently pushed away. "I don't want this anymore," she whispered aloud and was shocked to realize that she meant it. Looking out into the distance gave her a sense of the size of the lake; its grandeur and endless beauty felt too much somehow. She wanted something for herself, not the vastness before her, but the closeness of a kindred spirit. She wanted the feel of a soft hand holding her own, and she wanted to see love in another's eyes and all that comes with it.

It had now been a week since she had returned from her last visit with Simone and the absence of her touch left Vivian feeling hollow. She wanted so much to see her again. All her life she had felt a pull toward something grand. Following in her father's footsteps as an anthropologist had never been in question; it was what she wanted since childhood. To make her parents proud had always meant the world to her and it still did. That goal had been enough; up until recently, it had meant everything. However, the manifestation of her dreams, the dream that led her to another time and place, had changed everything. Meeting Amidah had changed everything and it could not simply be serendipity. No, it felt so much more than that; it felt as if it were fate. Amidah had opened a world to her like no other she could have imagined, and, in this world, she had found Simone.

She smiled now, a soft gentle movement of her mouth as she visualized Simone's large brown eyes. Simone, intelligent, witty, beautiful, and kind Simone. She was an independent successful woman, all the amazing attributes that Vivian admired and respected. She had never dared to believe that she'd be lucky enough to find someone who would touch her heart with such joy. She had discovered that life wasn't simply putting one foot in front of another; apparently, you could step sideways as well. Who knew? Feeling the mild pangs of loss, Vivian touched her heart with her hand. "I miss you, Simone. How has this happened? How can I be so invested in you so quickly? This is something I never anticipated." She continued to speak softly. "Yet here I am, sharing my heart with the surf and the clear skies, wishing that I could see you, hold you and share my heart because I'm in love with you."

CHAPTER 13

"Pick up, pick up, Annie," Simone whispered frantically as she bounced around on the balls of her feet. "Thank God!" she breathed out once she heard her sister's voice. "What are you doing right now? Can I come by the shop?" Simone paced her small balcony, coffee in hand, having just finished a long conference call. She had been very anxious to speak with her sister. She had had a dream last night that couldn't be anything but Vivian reaching out to her. She couldn't wait to tell her sister. Perhaps Annie would have some input.

"What is it? You sound out of breath. What? You want me to interpret a dream? Simone, honey, I don't...okay, yes, of course you can come by. I'll order us some lunch. Yes, okay. Bye-bye."

Simone disconnected the call with her sister and held her cell-phone to her chest. She felt a bit desperate and she knew that she sounded it as well. Poor Annie, she probably thinks her big sis has lost her mind. "Fuck it! This is too important, I'll explain every-thing to her once I see her," she said aloud. Grabbing what couldn't possibly be Amelia Earhart's jacket from the hall closet and her bag, she headed for her car and Annie's shop.

*   *   *

"I ordered us Thai. That's okay, right?" Annie said, placing the containers of steamy, fragrant food on her desk. "Hope you're hungry. Yum Thai makes the best hot curry chicken. Take a seat, sis. Oh, wait, grab two waters, will you please?" While Simone walked the short distance to the fridge, Annie looked at her closely. "Simone, what did you do differently?" Simone raised her eyebrows and looked at Annie. "You look amazing. I mean, don't get me wrong, you always look great, but I can't put my finger on it. Did you do something to your hair?"

Simone laughed. "It's the jacket. It might have belonged to Amelia Earhart. And, well, whenever I put it on it, it gives me a more confident appearance. I feel it does anyway," she said, shrugging her shoulders. It was now time for Annie to raise her eyebrows questioningly.

Ignoring Annie's gaze, she opened the small fridge and grabbed two bottles of water, handing one to Annie. "I had another dream. I mean, it's the first since Vivian left, uh, disappeared last week. I need your help to decipher it. Can you? Help me, I mean?" Simone watched her sister carefully as she dished out the food. She saw that Annie bit her lip, a sure sign that she was about to tell her something she did not want to hear. Plopping down into Annie's guest chair, she sighed, "You can't help me, can you?"

Simone continued to watch her sister and, just for a moment, a fleeting moment, she thought she'd scream. "I want more than anything to help you, to tell you what you want to hear, but I simply can't. I'm sorry; I have no point of reference for such things." Annie's face nearly made Simone cry; her sincerity could not have been more visible.

Clearing her throat, Simone reached for her plate. "You are

helping me, Annie. Just being able to come by to see you gives me comfort."

Driving home after lunch, Simone thought about her conversation with her sister. Despite Annie's insistence that she couldn't help her, she had. Simply being able to share her dream with someone she trusted, someone who believed that Vivian and she were destined to meet, gave her hope that they would be together again. Simone had shared nearly every detail of her dream with her sister, that of Vivian on a beach in a cove hidden from the shore, with her blond locks whipping around her face as she impatiently brushed them away. Simone had smiled at that; she already knew that Vivian was inpatient with her unruly blond tresses. She told Annie how Vivian had whispered the words out loud that she herself felt. "I'm in love with you."

Opening the door and stepping into her living room, Simone exhaled a long breath. She still could not get over how Vivian's presence, a mere week ago, had made her small condo so much more alive, so much more of a home. Smiling, she thought about how Vivian had been so curious about everything. Simone had found it adorable. She was more than willing to explain and answer all of Vivian's questions about the year 2023. After all, a hundred years was a great deal of time to travel through. 1923, Vivian was from 1923. Simone believed it now; she knew that it was real. However, she still found it incredible and miraculous that their meeting had happened, that they could touch each other, see each other and be in one another's presence. She did not pretend to understand it. Hell, if Annie and Maggie had not trusted her, she might have believed she had lost her mind.

The sound of her cell pulled her out of her thoughts. "Hello. Yes, I can come to the lobby. Okay, I will be down shortly. Yes, thank you." Grabbing her condo key, she wondered who would send her a package that required her signature? Well, she would soon find out. Reaching the lobby, Simone signed for her package. It was a thick envelope with no return address. Curious now, she quickly headed back upstairs and tore open the envelope. A folded scrap of paper floated to the floor. Quickly retrieving it; she began to read it.

Dear Simone,

I hope this note finds you well my dear. Enclosed you will find a notebook. The notebook arrived just yesterday as part of an archaeological dig from the 1920s. It is my understanding that the dig resulted in a very lucrative find for the museums sponsoring the expedition. However, this book was deemed not necessary to the original expedition. Therefore, it came to Metamorphosis to be auctioned off as a rare book find.

While preparing the notebook for auction, I discovered that the inside back cover included a photograph of two young women, which is, in itself, astonishing, as it is in pristine condition. However, what struck me even more is that the photograph also clearly includes the trunk you purchased. The detail cannot be replicated as the trunk is surely one of a kind. Therefore, based on this find, I felt it only prudent to forward it to you as part of your original purchase.

Best Regards,

Henry

Simone was flabbergasted. She could not believe what she held in her open palm. She looked at the notebook she held for only a moment before concluding it was a dig journal; Vivian's dig journal. She could not mistake it for anything else. Flipping through it, she noted it held Vivian's neat script and small, precise drawings. Most astonishing was that it was dated a year after Vivian arrived in Southern Kenya. More importantly, it was from a year in Vivian's future. Trying to wrap her brain around what this could mean, she walked to the kitchen holding the soft leather-bound notebook close to her heart. Sitting at her kitchen island, she huffed out a cleansing breath before opening the book to the back inside cover.

The photograph could have been taken yesterday. It was a rare color photo and, like the others pinned to the inside lid of the trunk, it was in excellent condition. Simone looked closely at the smiling faces of two women. The caption read, Port of New York, May 1921, Alex and Vivian. Simone saw that Vivian had clearly been preparing to board a ship. Standing next to her was a beautiful woman, tall and aristocratic and, just on the other side of Vivian, stood the trunk.

Going back to the first page of the journal, she began to read. According to Vivian's entries, she had left Southern Kenya after her eight-week stay, believing that her findings and follow-up reports from the expedition were secure and in the hands of the museum and university that hired her. However, that wasn't the situation at all. Later entries showed that she was in a court battle with a Dr. Escabar who had apparently taken credit for her work with the assistance of a colleague of his from the museum board who had helped to plagiarize her reports.

As Simone read further, the entries became more alarming. Apparently, this Dr. Escabar was very close to winning the court case, discrediting her and doing serious damage to her reputation and life's work. Vivian feared her career was close to being ruined.

Simone sat back and tried to think. She and Vivian had discovered that their time periods were synched in days and months. If Vivian's timeline held true, the journal she held in her hand was written one year in Vivian's future, a future that was possibly not yet set in stone. If she could warn Vivian somehow about what was to happen, perhaps Vivian could intervene and stop this Dr. Escabar from succeeding. Escabar's scheme has not yet happened she

The Trunk

theorized. Standing, she began to pace. "Fuck," she said, "I need to warn her." Somehow, she had to reach Vivian to tell her what Escabar was planning. But how? How was she going to tell her what was to come? Reaching for her cell, she called Annie. There had to be something that they could do.

* * *

"I know a woman."

Simone looked at Annie skeptically. "You know a woman? What does that even mean?" Simone had gone straight to Annie's shop the next morning and told her everything that had transpired the day before, beginning with the note from Henry, Vivian's journal entries, and the details about the man who was attempting to steal Vivian's work, ruin her reputation and destroy her career.

"Yes, I mean I know of her. I have never actually met her. But she is special, Simone." Simone watched as Annie rifled through her desk drawer, looking for what she had no clue. "Ah! Here it is." Holding up a small scrap of paper, Annie beamed at Simone. "Big sis, this woman apparently has gifts that we mere mortals cannot even comprehend. She may be able to help you get in contact with Vivian."

Despite her skepticism, Simone felt she had no other choice but to go with Annie's recommendation. What the hell, she was desperate and had nothing to lose at this point. If there was any chance, even the slightest chance, of contacting Vivian to warn her, she had to take it.

Sitting next to Annie and Maggie in the front seat of Annie's work truck might not have been the best idea. The old Chevy hit every bump and pothole in the road and trying to navigate using her cell's GPS was sketchy at best. Since they were somewhere

144

down in southern Illinois, Simone assumed the signal was about as good as it was going to get.

"Uh, tell me again why we decided to use your work truck instead of my car? Was I not thinking straight?" Bouncing around next to her, nearly knocking heads with Simone, Maggie nodded her agreement.

"Because, big sis, I have a full tank of gas and your fancy ride is electric. I doubt there are any charging stations where we are headed."

Looking at Annie, Simone responded, "My dear, sweet, knuckleheaded sister, my car is a hybrid, not electric. It takes gasoline."

Ignoring her sister's indignation, Annie said, "What does the GPS say is the next turn? I feel as if we've been on this stretch for hours. I didn't realize how far away this place is."

"Annie, where did you say this mysterious and amazing visionary is located? Mississippi?" Maggie sarcastically quipped.

Trying not to fear that their last-minute excursion may have been a mistake, Simone spoke, "Okay you two, let's get serious. The GPS says we have another 2.5 miles before you veer right onto Route 68. Then, from there, it's another two miles until the turn. After that, it's only a quarter of a mile up the road." Looking out the window of the truck's cab, Simone saw the late afternoon sun was starting to set; it would be twilight by the time they arrived. "Are you certain that this woman is expecting us so late in the day? I mean it seems an unusual time to visit a...what did you call her again?"

"Simone, please don't get cold feet now," Annie said soothingly, turning momentarily to Simone as she spoke, "I spoke with her housekeeper personally earlier today, and yes, she is expecting us. As far as what she is, well...I'm not quite certain. Apparently, she's from a remote area of Kenya. It's my understanding that she descends from a long prestigious line of seers. She is quite well known, yet very private. We are fortunate that she will even see us."

"How do you know her?" Maggie asked, now intrigued by what Annie had just shared. Simone also wanted to know how her sister knew who to contact. She briefly considered what other things she didn't know about her little sister. Both women looked at Annie as she drove, curiosity clearly etched on their faces.

"Well, let's just say I have my sources and leave it at that." Huffing out a sigh, Simone sat back, crossed her arms, and looked out the window at the sun setting over the horizon. Slowing the truck as they eased into a narrow dirt lane, Annie smiled and stated the obvious. "Ladies, we have arrived." Once Annie put the truck in park, Simone opened the door, got out, and stretched her cramped legs. Right behind her, Maggie did the same. Both women did a quick scan of their surroundings. Joining them, Annie stood next to Simone. "Wow."

Wow indeed. If Simone didn't know any better, she would have believed she was on a tropical island instead of rural southern Illinois. The small house was clad in white stucco with bamboo flower boxes decorating each window. Colorful blooms adorned the boxes, many of which Simone was certain did not grow in the midwestern United States. The thatched roof was pitched just enough to make it enchanting, and a nautical weathervane at the top of the roof turned slowly in the evening breeze.

"Alright, guys, let's go meet Amidah," Annie said as she began walking up the dirt lane.

Stopping in her tracks, Simone stood stark still. "What did you say?" she whispered, looking incredulously at her sister.

"I said, let's go meet Amidah. That's her name. I don't have a last name, but the woman I spoke with told me that is her name."

Simone began to pace.

"Simone? What is it?" asked Maggie.

Simone's heart was pounding hard and she was feeling a bit lightheaded. Amidah, Vivian's Amidah. Could it be one and the same? Impossible and yet, why not? Why would this be impossible? Looking up, she saw that both Maggie and Annie were waiting for her. Taking a deep breath, she put one foot in front of the other and followed them both down the lane.

Walking into Amidah's house was like being wrapped in a warm blanket in the dead of winter. Simone felt enfolded in a layer of comforting warmth. She knew that Maggie and Annie felt the same way as well, as the looks on their faces held awe and contentment. As it was dusk, the setting sun lent a mysterious tone to their surroundings. Everything appeared awash in various shades of orange and yellow, like an old-time sepia-tone photograph.

"Which of you is Simone?" The three women turned at the sound of a beautifully deep, accented voice. Standing in shadows across the foyer was a very tall, slightly stooped woman, dressed in colorful shades of bronze and red.

"I am," she said. Simone walked forward and slowly followed her.

*   *   *

Clearing her throat for the third time, Simone sat still and erect in a wooden chair and waited. The small leather journal suddenly felt heavy in her hands. She watched Amidah, who sat in a similar chair near the only window in the room with her hands folded on her lap and her eyes closed as if in prayer. She had been there, in Amidah's presence, for several minutes. She wasn't sure if she should speak and explain why she had sought out her help or simply wait until Amidah spoke. She decided to wait. This was her chance, she reasoned, to help warn Vivian. Oh, please, let this be my chance. She was certain now that Amidah knew everything anyway. She told herself she need only wait. So, she did. She closed her eyes and waited.

"Why have you come, child?" Simone was startled by the sudden sound of the clear deep voice. She had grown comfortable with the silence.

"I…I must, I mean, I need to make contact with someone. A woman, a traveler, she is far away." Biting her lip, Simone looked down at her feet, her nervousness making her hold tightly to the small book. Clearing her throat, she continued. "I'm sorry, I am somewhat flustered. Please, I need a moment." Amidah nodded. Closing her eyes and slowing her breathing, Simone worked to calm her nervousness.

"My dear." Eyes opening wide at the sound of Amidah's clear soft voice, Simone listened. "Do not try and fathom the reason you have made your way to me. It is of no importance. Only know that I am here. I am not the traveler who you seek, I am only a guide on the traveler's journey. Your words will find their intended audience and it will be she who will make them her destiny. Now child, speak."

*　　*　　*

Feeling cramped in the small cab of Annie's pickup, Simone fidgeted. It was a long drive back to Chicago, nearly two hours. She was finding it nearly impossible to sit still. She wanted to stand, pace, and speak out loud. She needed to repeat each word that Amidah had said, as each turn of a phrase had offered such wisdom that she wanted to repeat them.

She needed to be alone with her thoughts to allow what Amidah shared to sink in, to penetrate, marinate, and make sense in a way that would allow her to truly believe that there was a real chance for her and Vivian to be together.

"Monie?"

Turning toward the sound of Maggie's voice, she realized both women were staring at her. Annie was turning constantly from watching the road to watching her and then back again. "Annie, please focus on the road. I'm fine, really," she said and turned to look out the window.

Maggie couldn't keep quiet any longer. "Simone? So, what did she say? You're killing us here. I mean the look on your face when she asked for you; I thought you'd faint right then and there."

Puffing out a breath, Simone looked at both women, bit her lip, and then spoke. "The woman that I met tonight, that woman…well…I believe I was meant to meet her. I don't know how this all works, but I know *who she is*," she said with certainty. "Okay, Vivian shared with me that when she began having dreams of the two of us meeting, she did not understand what was happening. That is until she traveled to Kenya and found Amidah. Amidah became her guide and confidant. Now it appears that she is my guide as well."

"Are you serious?" Maggie said as she looked at Simone incredulously. "You're telling us that this woman is from Vivian's time? How is that even possible? I mean…she's here. We just met her for chrissake!"

Simone had no explanation. All she knew was that, since Florida, nothing seemed impossible. "I can't explain it. All I know is that when Vivian and I talked, she spoke of Amidah with awe and reverence, and today, I met her. She knew me, knew of me. Meeting Amidah has given me the strength I need to believe that Vivian and I are meant to be together, that she is the one I have waited for my entire life." Looking at Maggie, she could not help the emotion in her voice, an emotion so heartfelt that it overtook her, and she struggled to speak. "Through some sort of twist of fate, through a reality we cannot define, we have made our way to each other."

*   *   *

Tossing and turning Simone tried to sleep but knew that it wasn't going to happen. Getting out of bed, she walked to the living room, looked around, and then turned and walked into the kitchen. Standing in the dark room, she cursed out loud. This was driving her crazy, this not knowing what was going to happen. She had always considered herself a patient person, but this waiting to find out if, and when, Vivian would receive her message was nerve-racking. And, what of this Escabar person? Would Vivian be successful in stopping him from claiming her work as his own?

What frightened her the most was, after all of this, would Vivian return? Would she find her way back to her? Her assuredness that they were meant to be together was strong, yet this uncertainty of whether it would actually happen was exhausting and frightening.

The ice in her glass cracked as the strong liquid hit the frosty cubes. She had poured herself two fingers of whiskey. She hadn't had any since she shared a glass with Vivian. Tonight, she wanted to feel that burn in the pit of her stomach. She wanted the harsh liquid to ease her tension enough to think rationally. Rationally, there isn't anything remotely rational about what was happening. Putting down the whiskey, she reached for a throw and walked out to her balcony.

The chilly autumn wind hit her hard. Wrapping the throw

tightly around her, she looked at the clear evening sky and she felt a sudden pain. It was not a physical thing but it nearly knocked her over. "Vivian." Now, looking at the stars, she said her name again. "Vivian, please come back to me. Our strange, beautiful meeting means something honey, it must, something big and powerful, and not of this earth, but of eternity. Please, come back to me." Suddenly, feeling exhausted, she moved to her lounge and wearily laid down.

*   *   *

The frantic pounding woke her up with a start. Jumping up from the lounge, she made her way to the source of the furious knocking. Bleary-eyed from crying and lack of sleep, she looked through the peephole to see both Annie and Maggie standing in the doorway. It was clearly morning. Exhausted, she must have fallen asleep on her balcony last night. As she opened the door, they rushed into the room.

"There you are!" cried Maggie. "We have been trying to reach you since last night. What the hell, Monie? You want to give us a collective heart attack? I could kick your ass!" Clearly upset, Maggie went in search of coffee, leaving Annie alone with Simone.

Annie looked at Simone with sadness mixed with relief. Nodding in Maggie's direction, Annie half smiled, "You know how she gets. She was worried. We have been trying to reach you since we dropped you off yesterday. We tried hard to give you space, but it got to be too much for us so, this morning, we decided to come by to check on you ourselves."

"Dammit, where the hell do you keep the fucking coffee?" Both women cringed at the sound of Maggie's agitated voice coming from the kitchen.

"I think we better go in there before she trashes the place. You know she gets irritated when she's worried."

Simone nodded, realizing that she had been so self-absorbed that she had forgotten that both Annie and Maggie supported and loved her. They were a part of this fantastic adventure and she needed to include them. Simone walked into the kitchen and looked at Maggie's agitated face. Walking up to her she reached for her hand, "Maggie, Annie…please let's sit. I'll make us some coffee in a minute. I'm sorry. I know that I worried you" Simone said. "It's just that yesterday was incredibly surreal for me. I needed time to process what was happening…what *is* happening, I should say." Clearing her throat, Simone continued. "I mentioned to you both that Amidah is someone I know…well, know *of* actually. You see, Amidah is part of Vivian's world, from Vivian's time as far as I know. Vivian shared with me that Amidah is a very powerful seer, a Laibon actually, who descends from a long line of powerful shamans in east Africa. She is Vivian's guide, the person who helped Vivian navigate through her world to ours."

"When we arrived yesterday and Annie said the name Amidah, well, I freaked out. I knew then and there that meeting her was not simply random." Standing now, Simone paced the room. Stopping suddenly, she looked at both women. "Vivian and I have a connection. I feel it in my soul. We are destined to be together; I just know it. I have no clue how this all works, how a person from a hundred years in the past and clearly of another space…another parallel earth, could be my soul mate, but she is. I promise you she is, I just need to wait. Vivian must make the next move." Sighing heavily, she sat down and rubbed her eyes. "Do you think I've lost my mind?" she asked vulnerably.

Moving to Simone and throwing her arms around her friend, Maggie held her tightly. "Well, maybe a little," she said. "Oh,

Monie, seriously, of course we don't think you've lost your mind. We believe you." Jumping up, Annie threw her arms around both women and enthusiastically nodded her agreement. Simone had never felt so supported, yet her heart hurt terribly thinking of Vivian and, hoping against hope, that she would come back to her.

CHAPTER 14

The walk to the compound was difficult this early morning. Amidah could feel it in her legs, today more than yesterday. The sharp pinches to her knees and calves, and the slight pricks of pain, made each stride feel heavy and laborious. Slowing her pace, she wondered when she had gotten so old. Chuckling to herself, she shook her head. She knew time was catching up with her. Actually, sometimes she felt as if time had not only caught up with her but tackled her and left her in the dirt. Sighing, she was aware that soon she would not be able to make the short trip to the compound. Perhaps tomorrow she would stay at the village and allow her people to pamper her as they always wished. A small smile creased her lips; she would not allow that to happen. It was only a fleeting, selfish thought. Being pampered was never anything she wanted or needed.

Memories flooded her now like a brook after a heavy rain. As a girl, she had always wished to be a warrior like the young men of her village; she had been strong and full of fire with a heart of a lion. She had the youthful glow of promise and honor. She recalled how the young men of her village, and even a few young women, had admired her strength of personality and physical beauty.

"Ahh," she said to herself as she walked. "Old woman, you must stop. Those days have come and gone, and, as fate would have it; the life of a warrior was not your path." Though she had embraced her role as the wise Laibon of her people with grace and honor, it was a duty she would have preferred not to have been bestowed upon her those many years ago.

Looking ahead, Amidah saw the compound in the distance. She was nearly there. Smiling at the sun in the early morning sky, she thanked the gods for their blessings. "Ahh, Amidah, you are a silly old woman," she said as she laughed lightly, "Your memories are sweet, but now is not the time to dwell on them." Moving on from her reminiscences, she thought of Simone, the young woman she had recently visited, the woman who lived in a different world. Simone, so earnest and so eager to help Vivian. "Ahhh, love," she said, shaking her head with a bit of wistfulness. Waving her hand as if to dismiss her own memories once again, she walked on. "Yes, Simone, I will pass your warnings on to Professor Vivian, and, with your assistance, she will make the decisions that will determine the rest of her life, and quite possibly, yours as well."

*   *   *

"What? Amidah, I don't understand." Vivian looked up astonished. She was sitting on her cot, lacing up her boots and preparing for her early morning start when Amidah appeared at her tent flap and spoke in her strong yet soft voice.

"May I sit? This morning I am afraid I am feeling my age." Vivian jumped up and brought the camp chair closer to where Amidah stood. Slowly making her way, Amidah's tall frame sank into the well-worn canvas.

"Yes," she said after a deep sigh, "I have met your Simone."

Looking up into a stunned, hopeful expression, Amidah continued. "I have done something I rarely do; however, I felt that the
short journey I made was necessary. I am your guide, and, as such,
it is my duty to guide you." Amidah placed a small notebook on
Vivian's camp table. "I have been asked to give this book to you;
it is from Simone." Lifting herself from the chair, Amidah stood
and moved to where Vivian had haphazardly thrown her dirty
clothes. She carefully picked them up one at a time and put them
over her arm. "I will take these to the women to be laundered, if
you will excuse me, my child."

"Wait!" Vivian literally jumped to block Amidah's exit. "I mean,
please, a moment. You visited Simone? You went to her world, her
time?" Moving from the tent entrance Vivian paced slowly. "Why?
I mean how? No, please do not answer that question." Looking at
Amidah with wonder, she half-smiled. "How is she? Is she
well…did she ask after me?" Vivian's voice was soft, a bit melancholy and anxious.

Amidah looked closely at Vivian. She saw hope, love, and fear
in her eyes. She knew then that visiting Simone was the right decision. "She cares for you a great deal. Like you, she feels a deep
connection. You are the traveler, the one who must choose. I will
leave you now."

Rubbing her forehead, Vivian had no clue what was happening.
She needed to think…really think. Sitting back down on her cot,
she paused and tried to calm herself. She rechecked her bootlaces,
squirmed into her shirt, and finally stood up. Looking around, she
saw the small notebook that lay on the table. Reaching for it, she
now remembered that Amidah had placed it there. She had been
so focused on what Amidah was saying that she had not fully pro-
cessed that she had left the notebook. It was a small book and
looked very much like the kind that she herself used to journal her

dig notes. However, this one was not familiar. She had never seen this journal. Curious, she picked it up and opened it. It was dated a year in the future. "What in the world?" she exclaimed. There was a folded slip of paper tucked into the notebook. Taking it, she unfolded it and read.

My dearest Vivian,
I pray this notebook reaches you. It is fate that it has landed into my hands, I truly believe this. Your Amidah is quite formidable, and I trust her as I trust you. Be safe my love, I believe in you, and I know you will succeed. I am sending you my heart until we see one another again.
Simone

She held the note close to her heart and closed her eyes. After a moment, she refolded it and gently tucked it into her shirt pocket. Picking up the notebook, she slowly began to read. Immediately she saw that the writing was her own. The journal was clearly hers. Catching her breath, she plopped back down on her cot. Dear God, what is going on?

*   *   *

Stunned and bewildered, she reread the journal for the third time. For the third time, she studied each word, each line, each sentence. For the third time, she swallowed what felt like a peach pit lodged in her throat. Sitting at her small desk, she rubbed her forehead. The heat of the morning had quickly made itself known. Perspiration dripped down her spine, coated the crevasses behind her knees, and ran down her eyelids to the bridge of her nose. She sat, completely mesmerized by the words, until a drop of perspiration splashed onto the page that she held open. Startled, she came back to herself, to who she was now.

She needed to think. A journal, yet to be written by her, had been given to Amidah by Simone, one hundred years in the future. Simone, through some unknown source, was able to breach time and the mysterious phenomena of dimensions to warn her that Escabar, sometime in her near future, would steal her work and take full credit for himself. And, according to the yet-to-be-written journal, he would succeed. She would be discredited and the position she so desperately coveted at the University of Chicago would forever be out of reach.

If she was not living this reality, she would not have believed any of it would be possible. However, she was living it at this very moment and she needed to think. What was it that Amidah had said to her a day or two ago? Vivian had been standing, her hands on her hips, watching the small children of the village joyfully playing with a ball that one of the students had given them. Amidah had appeared behind her; she hadn't even heard her approach. She hadn't turned to look; she simply knew Amidah was there. Her words were soft, yet powerful, and Vivian knew that they were specifically and solely for her ears. "Do not concern yourself with why, it is of no consequence. Move forth to your life, the life you are destined to live, and the answers you seek will be made known."

*   *   *

Sitting in the back of the transport truck, she held tightly to the roll bar and prayed she was not too late. It was only a few miles to the main village where there was a train depot, shops, and supplies, but more importantly, a telegraph office. She needed to reach Rafael immediately. Blessed, loyal, brilliant Rafael. She knew that he could help her, there was no doubt in her mind. He was on every board and he knew everyone in the world of science, anthropology, and archeology. She had to depend on his expertise and, most importantly, his loyalty to her. She had no other choice. Jumping off the transport truck and making her way quickly through the throngs of people, she knew she had only a short period of time before the transport would head back to camp. She had to get the message off to Rafael immediately; there was absolutely no time to waste.

According to the journal, Escabar had quickly realized that her research and findings would be key to the entire expedition. In his mind, he could not allow that to happen; a woman credited with the findings of such importance was ridiculous in his purview. As the head of the expedition, he had to be the one person to receive the prestige of the findings. It was he alone who could move the department to heights that had never before been seen. So, with the assistance of one of his like-minded student interns, and a colleague at the university, Escabar had devised a plan to plagiarize her work and present it as his own. He had intercepted the documents she had forwarded to the university and was, Vivian feared, most likely retyping each detailed finding in his own words at that very moment. His goal was to send the documents to the university under his name, along with a lengthy review discrediting her work and painting her as difficult, uncooperative, and vindictive. Unfortunately, due to his previous successes and tenure, the university and museum board would agree, and she would be dismissed, and her reputation destroyed.

Reaching the telegraph office, Vivian was relieved to see that there was only one other person in line. Making her way to the counter, she carefully dictated enough information in the telegram to prompt Rafael to set the process in motion. She knew he would find out all that he could about Escabar and his questionable dealings, thus adding credibility and the necessary proof required to stop him from succeeding. She told him to expect more updates from her over the next few days.

Heading back from town, she breathed an uneasy sigh of relief. Sitting in the back of the truck, she allowed herself to be lulled by the easy landscape and warm African winds. Thinking back to the days of their early youth, she smiled; she, Alex, and Rafael had always connected. They had known one another for nearly fifteen years. Rafael will come through.

The sun was beginning to set once they had reached camp and, during the ride back, she had perfected the plan she had begun immediately after she read her journal. She knew she would need Mary Elizabeth's help to succeed. Mary Elizabeth mistrusted Escabar as much as she did. Yes, she'd speak with her first thing in the morning. Jumping off the transport truck she headed to her tent to grab her towel and toiletries. She needed a cool relaxing bath to help wash away the day and to calm her nerves. Stopping abruptly, she thought she saw someone heading away from the direction of her tent. She could not make out who it was. "Excuse me! Hey, you there!" she called. She lost sight of the person. Whoever it was had run into the thicket behind the bath tent and disappeared. "What the hell?" she said.

"Vivian?" Vivian turned and saw Mary Elizabeth quickly making her way toward her. "What's wrong? I heard you shouting." Mary Elizabeth looked concerned, and Vivian immediately felt relief at seeing her.

"I just saw someone making their way from my tent. Do you think Escabar sent him? Oh, this is so unbelievable. What next?" Clearly frustrated, she began to pace. Stopping abruptly, she spoke. "Mary Elizabeth, can I speak with you? Do you have a moment?"

Nodding, Mary Elizabeth reached for Vivian's arm, and they

walked the short distance to the shoreline. Waves crashed against the rocks and the faint sound of the villagers could be heard through the breeze.

"Tell me, did you see the person at all? Do you know who it was?" Mary Elizabeth looked around the immediate area, concern etched on her face.

"No, no I didn't get a clear look. He disappeared into the bush. Honestly, I'm not even certain he was in my tent. It appeared as if he saw me before he could enter and got spooked. But listen," Vivian said, more focused now on what she wanted to share with her, "I have something much more urgent to discuss." Looking at Mary Elizabeth, she felt grateful that she could trust her. "I have received some information regarding Escabar and it is not good. I can't help but think about the warning you gave me regarding his scheming ways and underhandedness." Vivian paced as Mary Elizabeth waited for her to continue. "I've heard, through great authority, that he is now, at this current moment, in the process of trying to plagiarize my work and discredit me as well. He has somehow intercepted my documents which, as you know, I had sent by currier to be delivered to both the university and head of the museum. I believe that they are still somewhere here in camp, I would stake my life on it, and I intend to get them back. I don't know how he managed it; my source has informed me that he has a co-conspirator amongst the team who is working with him and another one at the university."

"What? How do you know this? Never mind, I'm sure it's true," Mary Elizabeth whispered as she looked at Vivian incredulously. "That rat bastard! I knew he was up to something! This does not surprise me in the least." Now, it was Mary Elizabeth who was pacing. "He has ridiculed and worked to discredit female colleagues before. It is well known that he does not believe in women in science, that conniving idiot!" Turning to look at Vivian, Mary Elizabeth nodded and said, "Alright, what can I do to help?"

Looking at Mary Elizabeth, Vivian smiled. "You are something else, you know that?" smiled Vivian. "Alright then, I have a plan."

*   *   *

Vivian was nervous. She had shared her plan with Mary Elizabeth, who had suggested that they speak with David. Mary Elizabeth believed he would be a trustworthy ally and, quite honestly, they could use his credibility once Escabar's plan was made public. Vivian needed to get into Escabar's tent, locate her stolen work, and destroy any forgeries he may have created. She wasn't even certain he had her documents in his tent but, knowing the type of person he was, she trusted that he was keeping them close at hand. The plan was to get Escabar to join Mary Elizabeth and David in Mary Elizabeth's tent for cocktails. They would keep him occupied long enough to get him sufficiently intoxicated. This would give Vivian enough time to search his tent for her documents and, just as importantly, his plagiarized copies. Without the originals, he would have no way to rewrite her findings. Once she located the materials, she would contact Rafael, who would secure a courier to personally deliver the documents to the university and museum in New York.

Now, it was only a few hours until the end of the workday. The plan was for both David and Mary Elizabeth to talk up Escabar at the end of the work shift, stroke his ego, ask for his assistance, then immediately invite him for drinks, thus occupying his time with whiskey in order to give Vivian time to search his tent for her notebooks. Vivian had to remember to thank David for offering up his two prized bottles of Scotch for the cause. Hell, if this plan works, she'd buy him an entire case of Scotch. Once Escabar was safely preoccupied, Mary Elizabeth would signal Vivian.

Vivian was nervous but determined. She looked to the sky and thanked whatever gods had sent her Simone. If her plan succeeded, Simone was 100 percent responsible for saving her reputation and credibility. Lord, how she missed her. Not a day went by without Simone dominating her thoughts. Oh, how she longed to hear that amazing laugh and see that beautiful smile again. She had made a decision. If Simone would have her, if she agreed, Vivian would spend the rest of her life with her, in her world. Good heavens, it was frightening, but she knew in her heart that it was more frightening to be without her. The thought of leaving her beloved friends, Alex and Rafael, was heartbreaking, but she needed to move in the direction of her heart, and that meant life with Simone. Amidah had said that she needed to choose. For a long time, she didn't understand. Choose what? Well now she knew, and she chose love.

CHAPTER 15

Simone felt as if she were running for her life. It had now been five days since she'd had her encounter with Amidah and she had heard nothing. With her sneakered feet pounding the payment, she ran, consumed with thoughts of Vivian and her meeting with Amidah. It was making her crazy. Where were they? The day after she met with Amidah, she had tried to contact her by using the phone number which Annie provided her, but it had been disconnected. She had suspected this would be the case and was not at all surprised that it no longer worked.

Looking at her smartwatch, she was surprised to see that she had run over six miles. She needed to turn back as she had an important meeting that she needed to prepare for. Turning around, she thought she caught a glimpse of someone familiar. An old woman had turned the corner and disappeared. Following her, Simone turned the same corner quickly. However, there was no one, not a single soul walking down that street. She wondered if it could have been Amidah. Wiping the sweat from her brow, she turned and ran in the direction of home.

*   *   *

Sitting on her balcony, she watched the evening sky. The muted sounds of the traffic below slowly eased her tension. She was never one for silence; too much quiet unnerved her. Better to have white noise, and the sound of the city from her private space always seemed to help soothe her. The meeting had gone well and funding for the new shelter in Little Village had been secured. She should be celebrating, not moping. Hearing her cell ring, she knew it was Annie but she didn't feel like speaking with anyone right then. Annie and Maggie had been phoning her on and off since early morning. To appease their concern, she had texted them and told them she would speak with them tomorrow. Half smiling, she knew her sister well enough to know that her text had not stopped her from calling. Reaching for her phone, which continued to ring, she clicked on the call. "Yes, Annie," Simone said.

"Good, you answered. Sis, I saw your Amidah. I saw her in a dream I had last night. I would have told you earlier if you had answered your damn cell or checked your text."

Simone quickly responded. "Are you certain, that it was her? What did she say? Did Vivian receive my warning about that creep Escabar? Did she stop him? Is she coming back here, to Chicago…to our time?"

"Slow down, sis, and let me get a word in, woman," Annie said exasperatedly.

"Sorry, please go ahead."

"She was walking a small dog of all things. Somewhere here in the city, near the lakefront, I think. Anyways, I saw her, and I ran after her but, the closer I thought I was getting, the farther away she seemed to be. She turned and smiled at me as if she were playing tag and she couldn't be caught. But what really surprised me was that she smiled broadly and, of all things, gave me the A-okay sign. I felt a sense of relief and I immediately wanted to call you to tell you that Amidah had delivered your message, the warning to Vivian."

Simone thought about what Annie just shared. She couldn't laugh off her sister's abilities any longer; they had been spot-on. Ever since she found Vivian, Annie had been at her side, strong and supportive. "I believe you. Thank you, hon; you are the best sister anyone could ever hope to have. Thank you." Sitting back down on her lounge, she closed her eyes and petitioned the universe that her message would arrive in time and that Vivian would be successful in stopping Escabar.

*   *   *

Sitting on a stool in front of her tent, Vivian cleaned the mud from her work boots, the mundane chore made more tedious as she waited impatiently for Mary Elizabeth's signal. What was taking so long? David had persuaded Escabar to join him and Mary Elizabeth for a drink in her tent. Now she could hear their loud laughter as Mary Elizabeth's old hand-cranked gramophone played Bessie Smith's soulful blues. Standing up and stretching to ease a crick in her back, she saw Mary Elizabeth place her own work boots outside the tent flap. Finally, the signal! The plan was in motion! Now she needed to make her way into Escabar's tent without being detected. "Shit," she said under her breath. There were a few staff milling around, as well as a couple of the team. She would need to be careful and inconspicuous. "Okay, Vivian, don't dawdle. You can do this," she said.

Without further delay, she placed her now mud-free boots back into her tent, walked out, and made a big show of looking around camp. Periodically, she waved to others who were milling about or heading toward their own tents. Slowly, she made her way toward the mess tent. Escabar's tent was a good two hundred feet north of it. She wanted to make it appear as if she were walking over to get tea or a snack. Thank heaven that it was dusk and that the moon offered enough light so that she could make her way without the use of a torch or lantern. Finally, she was close enough to Escabar's tent to slip inside without being detected. Breathing a sigh of relief, she stood for a moment in the dark of his space to get her bearings.

"Okay, okay, get moving," she whispered. Without hesitating, she began to rummage through Escabar's desk and trunk. The evening light was dim but she could still make out how well-organized Escabar's belongings were. Damn, just my luck that this scoundrel is so neat. Placing everything that she had moved back into place so as not to be suspected, she continued to search. Panic began to seep in; she could feel the heat of the evening. Where the hell are they?

She could not locate her documents anywhere. Moving as best she could with minimal light, her foot caught. Looking closely, she realized she had nearly tripped over a thick strap that was sticking out from under Escabar's open trunk. Searching through the trunk resulted in nothing related to her documents. Frustrated, she reached down and tugged on the strap under the trunk, but it wouldn't budge. Attempting to move the trunk out of the way proved to be difficult as it was extremely heavy. Finally, after a couple of solid pushes, she was able to move the heavy trunk enough to notice that the ground under the trunk was disturbed. It looked as if it had been dug up. "What the hell," she whispered. She saw that the soil under the trunk was fresh and patted down. Quickly digging with her hands, she discovered a buried canvas bag. Unzipping the bag proved difficult as her hands were shaking badly and sweat dripped from her temple.

Finally, opening the bag, she saw what she came for; here were her documents, still in their leather pouch, along with several typed pages. It was her documents and Escabar's copies, she realized. She quickly placed the leather pouch and copies in her shirt, kicked the soil back over the hole, and pushed the trunk back to its original location. Just as she was about to leave the tent with her treasure, she heard Escabar stumbling toward her. "Shit!" she said, "Now what?" With no other option, Vivian crawled under Escabar's cot, moving as far back as possible while praying that he wouldn't see her. Holding the leather pouch against her chest, Vivian waited.

Belching loudly, Escabar stumbled into his tent. He was humming merrily and mumbling about how he knew that Mary Elizabeth had the hots for him. "Just you wait, Professor, I'm going to show you want a real man is like," he said as he belched again and then fell heavily onto his cot. The weight of his fall hit her shoulder and she unconsciously braced herself, ready to be discovered. But Escabar didn't move. Instead, Vivian heard loud snores and saw his foot flop over the side of the cot.

After waiting for what felt like an eternity, Vivian made her move. She knew she needed to get the hell out of there before he woke. But how? She was practically pinned by his weight and his foot blocked part of her exit. Thinking of Simone, she decided to just go for it. Simone will be so proud of me when I tell her this story. Lord, I hope I will have the opportunity to tell her this story. The sudden thought of Simone gave her the push she needed to make her escape. Looking at Escabar's extended leg, she knew she was going to have to move it; there was no other way to get past it. The majority of the cot was blocked by supplies and it would be much too noisy to try and move them. Taking a deep breath, she gently lifted his booted limb and quickly slithered free. Without a second thought, she crawled out of the tent and quickly made her way to her own tent on the other side of camp.

As planned, Mary Elizabeth and David were waiting. "Oh, thank goodness! There you are! We were beginning to panic. Are you quite alright? What happened?" Mary Elizabeth looked spooked and Vivian couldn't stop herself from hugging her.

"I'm fine. Look, I have it. I have it all, the documents, and Escabar's copies! He came stumbling into his tent just as I was about to make my exit. I had to hide under his cot. Luckily, he passed out quickly. I was lucky to get away."

"I knew the sleeping powder in his drink would do the trick," breathed out Mary Elizabeth with a gleeful laugh.

Breathing heavily with excitement and relief, Vivian looked at Mary Elizabeth with awe. Feeling a bit out of breath for a moment, she weaved slightly.

"Whoa there, Vivian! Are you alright?" David gently held Vivian's elbow to steady her.

Looking at David, she smiled and nodded. "Yes, I am…I am most definitely alright."

*   *   *

In the days following her successful retrieval of her documents from Escabar's tent, Vivian felt tense and edgy. Everywhere she went in camp, and at the dig site, Escabar watched her. He knew very well what she had done, yet he never said a word. She knew that he was attempting to intimidate her; it was uncomfortable and frightening. After all, she couldn't know if he would attempt to be violent with her at some point. At this juncture, his temper and arrogance were well known by all involved in the expedition.

Fortunately, she had David and Mary Elizabeth. Together they made a formable team, and Escabar had no choice but to act as if everything was status quo.

What Escabar didn't know, and would soon discover, was that his days were numbered. The very next morning following the retrieval of her documents, Vivian had contacted Rafael by telegraph, explaining in detail what had transpired. In addition, David and Mary Elizabeth contacted the museum and university, summarizing his treatment of the local people and members of his team, in addition to corroborating Vivian's story.

Now, nearly a week after Vivian, David, and Mary Elizabeth had foiled Escabar's plan, word had come down by telegraph to the senior team members that Escabar was to be suspended as director of the expedition, effective immediately, and that an investigation into all allegations was underway. The complaints from David Handler and Professor Smith regarding Escabar's treatment of the villagers were enough for the board to ask for an investigation. In addition, Rafael had come through as a board member of the Museum; his word was highly regarded. When he had brought Escabar's plan to plagiarize Vivian's work to the board of directors, they had no choice but to suspend Escabar. Mary Elizabeth, as the lead archaeologist, was placed in charge for the remainder of the expedition which would be winding down within the week. Escabar was summoned back to the States to face the consequences. The morning he was informed, he became infuriated and left camp before dawn. He was angry and petulant, kicking over chairs and nearly ripping down his tent before he boarded the transport truck that would take him to the ship and to his own destiny.

"Professor Vivian." Looking up from attempting to organize her belongings, Vivian smiled with genuine joy. She hadn't seen Amidah for over a week. Word around camp was that she had fallen ill. This terrified Vivian as she had grown to care a great deal for her. She was also aware that, as the spiritual guide of her people, no outsider could visit Amidah while she was convalescing.

With no contact from Amidah and believing she would not have any further contact with her prior to her journey back to the States, Vivian had been forced to conclude that this life, here in her world, would be her destiny. Being a well-respected professor and archaeologist with a splendid career was not really a bad deal, she reasoned halfheartedly. However, it was no longer the life she had yearned for; she wanted a life with Simone, in her world. Over the past several nights she had dreamed of her, her beautiful, dark-haired woman from another world, another dimension, and from a future so foreign to her that it boggled her mind.

"Amidah, you're here," she said, walking the short distance to embrace her. "How wonderful to see you, and to know you are well." Holding her gently, Vivian smiled. "It is good to see you. I have missed you."

"And I have missed you." Making her way slowly into Vivian's tent, she pointed to the only chair. Vivian quickly moved it closer so that Amidah could seat herself. Looking around the small enclosure, Amidah spoke. "I see you are preparing for tomorrow's early morning journey." Pressing her lips together tightly, Vivian shrugged her shoulders, her eyes glistening with tears. "Child, what is it? Why are you sad? Did you not succeed in your efforts to right a terrible wrong?" Amidah's soft kind eyes watched Vivian as she composed herself.

"Yes, yes, I am so grateful for the outcome. Not only was I spared, but so were my team members. Escabar's success would have been devastating for them as well." Turning to Amidah, Vivian plopped down on her cot and put her head down. Sniffing back her emotions, she spoke. "But is this life," she said as she looked around, "what I truly want? I thought it was, though that was before I met Simone and found the joy of another's love. I never believed that I'd ever experience love. I saw how happy and dedicated my parents were to each other. Oh, Amidah, they were so in love; even after many years, they were everything to each other. Yet they always had time for me. They loved me, involved me in their lives, and taught me to be compassionate and giving. They were amazing people."

Sniffling back tears, Vivian smiled sadly. "I want what they had. I believe that is my true destiny. I once believed it was only my father's success as an anthropologist that was the prize, the goal. However, because of what I feel with Simone, I now understand that there is so much more." Looking at Amidah, she spoke with conviction. "It is also their compassion, and dedication, their beautiful happy life together that I crave. I hadn't realized that truth until I met her. Now, well…I'm not certain I'll ever see her again." Vivian ran her fingers through her hair and took a deep breath.

"My child…Vivian?" Looking up from her misery, Vivian smiled.

"I have a gift for you. I should explain…it is very old. It is what is called in your language, a talisman. It will guide you on your true journey." Placing the object in Vivian's palm and closing her fingers over its smooth surface, Amidah smiled. "Believe in its truthfulness. Its power is your truth."

Vivian looked down at the object that rested in her hand and felt its strength resonate through her. It was like a cool breeze on a hot day. It felt crisp and fresh. Eyeing the talisman closely, she saw that it was intricately made. Small pieces of coral and shells adorned it and the colorful shells were intertwined with silver thread. A small bronze oval, dark and heavy, rested in the center of its detailed design. The ornament hung from a leather cord.

Placing the talisman around her neck, Vivian spoke, "Thank you, Amidah, I will cherish this gift and I will honor its truth; I give you my word." Her heart swelled with respect, admiration, and affection for this woman who had opened her eyes to a new brilliant reality. "You are an amazing person. I am so grateful to have had you in my life." Smiling, Amidah rose from the chair and slowly made her way toward the doorway of Vivian's tent.

"Farewell Professor Vivian, your journey has just begun." With those parting words, Amidah started back to her village, content in the knowledge that she had helped guide a fellow traveler.

Watching Amidah leave, Vivian was mesmerized. She seemed to be a goddess, a queen, or some other graceful, beautiful being. Amidah didn't simply leave a room; she made an exit. She glided out of the space in such a way that she left the observer speechless. Holding the talisman tightly, Vivian moved it close to her heart, praying that it would guide her as Amidah believed it would. "All my life, I have longed for something; I simply did not know what that something was that I longed for. I have always seemed to be searching. That was until I found Simone and with her, my future. Amidah, you said that my journey has only just begun. I pray that this is true."

The early evening sounds of Africa were making themselves known; birds, insects, and faraway beasts echoed their existence. Standing now in the doorway of her tent, Vivian took in the sounds that she had come to love. It was a beautiful evening, with a bit less heat and humidity. It was as if the land had given her a gift as well. Turning and making her way back into her space, she looked around. Her kerosene lamp created a soft glow in her small tent and she felt a sudden melancholy to be leaving this wild beautiful world that she had inhabited for the past two months. Sighing, she lay down on her cot. Looking at the talisman, she gently rubbed its smooth surface. "I haven't even completed my packing," she said to herself, as she looked around, "and we are leaving in less than six hours." No matter, there wasn't really anything that she wanted that could not be stuffed in her shoulder bag. Tired…she was so tired. Her eyes began to close and sleep was consuming her when she quickly jerked back awake. "No, I must not sleep. I need to prepare for tomorrow's early morning journey," she reminded herself. Yawning, she conceded, "Well, maybe if I just close my eyes for a few minutes." Still holding tightly to the talisman, she whispered Simone's name and felt the warm wrap of comforting arms around her. Succumbing to sleep, she didn't see the soft glow of the object she held so tightly to her heart.

CHAPTER 16

"Its power is your truth," Vivian whispered, half asleep. An abrupt cold wind made her shiver; her fingers were stiff and goosebumps had sprung up over her entire body. Waking up slowly, she curled up and wrapped her arms around herself trying to keep warm. Struggling to bring her brain to the present, she blinked. A momentary panic seized her. Had she missed her transport to the ship that would take her back to the States and her life? Gasping, she sat up with a start and a sudden comprehension moved through her. Her heart pounded with a joy that she had never experienced. A woman's surprised exclamation startled her, and she nearly tumbled from the lounge that had been her bed. And now, a warm embrace held her tightly against a soft bosom.

Needing to see her face, Vivian moved gently back from the embrace. Here was her Simone; her bright, beautiful eyes sparkling with surprise and delight, and her smile wide and welcoming. As she looked deep into Simone's eyes, she was certain that this is where she was meant to be, right here, right now, with Simone, in her world. "Simone…it's really, truly you, my darling, am I really here?" she said as she gently touched her cheek.

Moving into Vivian's touch, Simone smiled, her heart filled with deep joy. "Oh, sweetheart, I don't know how…but yes, you are really here!" Pulling Vivian close once more, Simone peppered her with soft kisses. "Oh, honey, I prayed every single day that Amidah was able to give you my message and my warning about this Escabar character. Please tell me that she was successful and that you were somehow able to stop him."

"Yes, my love, Amidah delivered the journal, and, with the help of some amazing friends, we were able to stop Escabar from succeeding. Thank you, my darling, thank you for everything."

Helping Vivian off the lounge, Simone guided her into the living room and covered her with a warm blanket, rubbing her arms for warmth. Vivian took in the feel of her surroundings, the softness of Simone's couch, the warmth and coziness of the room, and the feel of Simone warming her body.

"Vivian, baby, look at me please." Vivian lifted her head and looked directly into Simone's sweet loving gaze. "I love you, Vivian. I love you. Ever since I was a child, I knew that there was one special person for me, one person who would be my soulmate. I didn't understand it then. Honestly, I didn't understand it until I met you. Please stay with me, Vivian. Stay with me and I promise, we will be happy."

Looking at Simone, Vivian was filled with gratitude and love. Reaching for the talisman, secure around her neck, she held it gently in her hand and silently thanked Amidah for helping her know her own truth. She knew now that this magnificent woman, who held her with such tenderness, was her destiny. Whatever their lives encountered in this new world she had chosen, she believed that with Simone, she would prevail.

"Simone," she said smiling, "I will never leave you again. A life with you is what I choose." Reaching over, she pulled Simone to her and kissed her deeply. "I love you. I will love you forever," she whispered.

*   *   *

Waking from a long deep sleep, Vivian felt refreshed and energized. Yawning, she turned slightly, and her heart swelled as she watched Simone sleep; her eyelids lightly fluttered, and her soft breathing was easy and calm. Reaching over, she gently touched Simone's cheek. Seeing her eyes slowly open from the touch of her hand, she smiled. "I'm still here," she whispered.

"I was afraid you might not be," Simone whispered back. "How do we know you won't disappear again? Honestly, I don't think I could bear it if you did."

"Darling, please believe me. I know. I feel it deep in my chest, in my heart, that I will never leave you again. I don't understand it, I don't know how our lives together are possible, but I know that it is. Amidah was part of our lives for a reason, and that reason was to bring us together." Smiling gently, Simone pulled Vivian into her arms and held her close.

"Yes, I believe you, honey. I do. However, it may take a few years of waking with you each morning for me to truly be comfortable." Simone joked. "Vivian," Simone said suddenly. "The university!"

"The university? What about it, I don't follow."

"The university, babe! Just maybe…okay," Simone said, now sitting up in bed and looking excitedly at Vivian. "When I first opened your trunk and found you, well, I researched you. Columbia University archives had you listed as a visiting professor, but nothing more. I wonder, I wonder if now, if now, there would be more information. Things have changed. You're here now and you stopped that Escabar character. Stands to reason your history has changed as well." Excitedly, Simone kissed Vivian on the lips and jumped out of bed. "Whatja say, honey, would you like to see?" she said, holding out her hand to Vivian.

*   *   *

"Oh, dear lord! Is this real?" Sitting at Simone's kitchen island with coffee and an untouched scone, Vivian stared at the words on Simone's laptop. No longer was there a short reference to Vivian's tenure at Columbia. Now there was an entire biography and history dedicated to her and, to both Vivian's and Simone's astonishment, a mystery that had apparently taken the world by storm. According to a lengthy exposé in *Time* magazine dated December 1923, Professor Vivian Oliver, a prominent anthropologist who had won praise and the respect of the anthropological world for her work documenting the previously little-known history of ancient peoples of Kenya, had mysteriously disappeared the day before she was to return to the States. A lengthy investigation and search of the area had been completed, resulting in no answers pertaining to her disappearance. Initially, there had been speculation that foul play was involved, however, in the end, the investigation led to a dead end.

"Simone! I disappeared. The day before I was to leave, that was yesterday, the day I arrived here in your world!" Sitting back in her chair, Vivian stared wide-eyed at Simone.

"Are you okay? Please tell me you have no regrets, because…" Simone asked. Vivian quickly threw her arms around her and held her close.

"Oh, darling, of course I don't. It's only that this is all quite extraordinary and surreal. To find oneself in a news article as a mystery, only to know exactly what occurred."

"Ugh, I'm sorry. Of course, I get it. I mean I can't relate obviously but, with all that has occurred these past months, I do understand how overwhelming it can be." Simone pulled Vivian onto her lap and held her. "I love you, Vivian. You are everything I didn't know I needed." Smiling at Simone, Vivian reached for her and kissed her passionately.

*   *   *

Sitting in front of Simone's small fireplace next to the woman she loved, comfortable and warm under a soft throw, Vivian considered the events of the day. From further research, they had discovered that she was quite famous. Her research in Kenya, and follow-up written analysis, had led to additional research over the years. That research had helped the people of the region cultivate their lands and preserve their way of life for generations to come. It was a heady realization for her, knowing that she was part of something grand. Still, the knowledge that she was a mystery, yet to be solved, was difficult to comprehend. She had disappeared, yet how strange to know that she knew exactly where she was. She hadn't really disappeared, in her purview, she had actually found her way home. "Yes, I am home," she whispered.

"What was that, my love?" Simone asked, clinking her wine glass with Vivian's. Smiling Vivian leaned into Simon and gently kissed her cheek.

"Oh, nothing, darling, I just said it's so good to be home."

EPILOGUE

Vivian stood back from the small crowd of mostly women. She watched Simone greet their guests and offer them wine. Smiling at the scene, she marveled at the freedom that women in this century enjoyed. Even after nearly two years with Simone, she could still be awestruck by sights that Simone took for granted. When she had first come to Simone's world to stay, they had talked early into the wee hours of the morning, excited to be together. They wanted to know everything about each other, their goals and their dreams, their likes and dislikes, and their fears. In the days and weeks that followed, they grew closer still, secure in the knowledge that being together, in Simone's world was right.

After the excitement of those first weeks together it was Simone who gently, but with a drive and dedication that truly impressed Vivian, aided her in establishing an identity that would not be questioned in her new world. It still, even after all these months, amazed her that, to the world, she was no longer Vivian Terese Oliver born December 17, 1893. Smiling, she recalled Simone's words when she shared with her that she was a bit melancholy about changing her identity; Simone had looked at her with such love and admiration, and whispered, "You, my love, will always be Vivian Terese Oliver, no matter where you land in the universe." Those words gave her a sense of happiness because she knew them to be the absolute truth.

It had taken time to build her a new history. It was astonishing to Vivian the limitless amount of knowledge on any subject one could obtain from what she quickly learned was known as the internet. They had begun initially by securing her a simple library card, under the name of a long-ago deceased Vivienne Richards from Illinois. Vivienne Richards had been born the same year as Maggie and had died at the age of ten when the bird flu killed her and her parents in her small rural town. Using her identity and a copy of her birth certificate, Vivian had opened a bank savings account at a small neighborhood bank where she'd gone several times with Simone. Finally, she was able to apply for a replacement social security card using Vivienne Richards's birth certificate and the other ID she had acquired. These steps proved tedious but invaluable to building her life here in her new reality. Now, well now, she was well on her way to reestablishing her career; due to her expertise in the field of anthropology, she was able to fast-track and obtain her master's degree. She did not plan on slowing down either; her next step would be her Ph.D. She smiled with the knowledge that she had her entire new life ahead of her and, most importantly, Simone would be at her side to share it.

"What are you thinking, Professor Vivian? You seem very deep in thought." Turning, Vivian smiled at Annie who now stood next to her offering her a glass of champagne. Vivian loved that Annie called her professor in such an affectionate way. She had recently secured a position at the University of Chicago as an adjunct professor; her destiny and dreams were coming full circle. How serendipitous, she thought, that her expert knowledge of the ancient peoples of Kenya's southern region would be exactly what the university's history department had been looking for. She did not wish to question her good fortune. Amidah would be proud that she simply accepted it as part of her destiny.

Accepting the glass of wine from Annie, Vivian smiled. "I'm thinking that I couldn't be happier than I am right at this moment."

"Well, my dear sister-in-law, I am still smiling from ear to ear every time I see you and Simone together. Honestly, I have never seen her so truly happy, so content." Reaching for Annie's hand, Vivian squeezed it with affection and gratitude.

"Thank you. She makes me just as happy and content." Hearing Simone laugh, she gazed her way. Looking at her never ceased to send a thrill down her spine. Smiling, Simone excused herself from their guests and walked the short distance toward Vivian and Annie standing near the open balcony door. A soft, warm breeze filled the room and the lights of the city, under the clear evening sky, were nearly picture-perfect.

Placing a sweet kiss on Vivian's cheek, Simone smiled mischievously. "Okay, what are you two whispering about over here? Are you sizing up the room to see which single women you can pair up or are you wondering which of our friends are going to try and hit on Maggie again?" All three women laughed, as it was well known amongst their crowd that the beautiful, blond-haired, tomboyish Maggie was straight. However, that fact did not appear to deter some of their single lesbian friends who never missed an opportunity to try and change Maggie's mind about her sexuality. As if their discussion had pulled her across the room, Maggie made her way toward the three women.

"Monie, your friend Sahnya from college wants to teach me to kayak. Isn't that sweet? She said that she has a beautiful two-person kayak at her home, not far from Chicago."

All three women looked at Maggie and burst out laughing. Looking a bit sheepish, and knowing too well when she was being teased, Maggie gently swatted Simone on the arm. "Oh, stop you three, I know that she's interested in me. She's been flirting with me all evening." Looking at Maggie now, they said nothing. "What?" Maggie asked. "Look at her, she's gorgeous, intelligent, and really sweet, and I have always wanted to learn to kayak. So, if you will excuse me, ladies." With that, Maggie winked, turned, and walked back to the makeshift bar where Sahnya stood waiting to replenish her glass.

Simone huffed out a laugh. "What the hell was that?" Both Annie and Vivian couldn't help but laugh at Simone's reaction.

Annie shook her head. "Well, hell, you go, Maggie," she said with a grin. "Besides, kayaking is fun!" Turning toward Vivian and Simone, she lifted her glass indicating that she too was going to get a refill. Both Vivian and Simone watched her as she walked toward the small group of women.

"You know darling, in my day it was said that if you continue to stand with your mouth open like that, you'll catch a fly." Turning toward Vivian, Simone closed her open mouth and smiled.

Lacing her fingers through Vivian's, Simone lifted her hand and kissed it gently. "Well, babe, apparently I can still be surprised and amazed."

Laughing, Vivian pulled her toward the balcony. "Come along, lovie, I want to kiss you desperately. I still have a few surprises of my own that will amaze you."

ABOUT THE AUTHOR

C.M. Castillo is a Chicago-based author of fiction focusing on strong, engaging characters, fantasy, hints of romance, and times past. Her debut novel, *The Pages of Adeena*, was published in 2019 and was awarded a finalist status in November 2020 under the LGBTQ fiction category sponsored by American Book Fest. C.M. worked as a featured columnist for *The Windy City Times*, Chicago's LGBTQ publication. *The Trunk* is her second novel. To learn more, visit www.cmcastillowriter.com.

9 781957 917061